The Sleepover Club

Three fantastic Sleepover Club
stories in one!

Have you been invited to all these sleepovers?

Mega Sleepover Club ④

Happy Birthday Sleepover Club
Sleepover Girls on Horseback
Sleepover in Spain

Fiona Cummings
Narinder Dhami

Collins

■ *An imprint of* HarperCollins*Publishers*

The Sleepover Club ® is a registered trademark of HarperCollins*Publishers* Ltd

Happy Birthday Sleepover Club first published in Great Britain by Collins 1998
Sleepover Girls on Horseback first published in Great Britain by Collins 1998
Sleepover in Spain first published in Great Britain by Collins 1998

First published in this three-in-one edition by Collins 2001

Collins is an imprint of HarperCollins*Publishers* Ltd
77-85 Fulham Palace Road, Hammersmith
London W6 8JB

The HarperCollins website address is www.**fire**and**water**.com

3 5 7 9 10 8 6 4 2

Happy Birthday Sleepover Club
Sleepover Girls on Horseback
Text copyright © Fiona Cummings 1998

Sleepover in Spain
Text copyright © Narinder Dhami 1998

Original series characters, plotlines and settings © Rose Impey 1997

ISBN 0 00 712844-4

Printed and bound in Great Britain by Omnia Books Limited, Glasgow G64

Sleepover Kit List

1. Sleeping bag
2. Pillow
3. Pyjamas or a nightdress
4. Slippers
5. Toothbrush, toothpaste, soap etc
6. Towel
7. Teddy
8. A creepy story
9. Food for a midnight feast:
   chocolate, crisps, sweets, biscuits.
   In fact anything you like to eat.
10. Torch
11. Hairbrush
12. Hair things like a bobble or hairband,
    if you need them
13. Clean knickers and socks
14. Change of clothes for the next day
15. Sleepover diary and membership card

Happy Birthday Sleepover Club

Collins

An imprint of HarperCollinsPublishers

CHAPTER ONE

BOO! It's me. Kenny. You were expecting Frankie, right? Well, she couldn't come. She's ill. Not really, really ill, unfortunately. I could do with a proper patient to practise on. You can't train to be a doctor by operating on your sister's stuffed toys. But all Frankie Baby has is a bit of a temperature and a sore throat. Nothing to worry about. And not surprising either. You know how she can go on sometimes.

Phew! I'll just sit down for a minute and get my breath back. I was practising a few cartwheels before I got to you. Did you see me? The thing with cartwheels is that all the blood rushes to your head, then you go all kind of dizzy. It's quite nice actually. I was doing cartwheels here in this park when we thought of having the Sleepover Club birthday party.

It was at the beginning of the summer holidays. I was with the rest of the Sleepover Club and I was bored. I was bored because there was no football. I *live* for Leicester City Football Club, and I hate it in summer when the season has finished. But it wasn't just me, we were all feeling a bit bored. It's really weird because all we'd talked about for the last few weeks at school was what a great time we were going to have during the school holidays. We'd be sitting in the classroom struggling over some stupid maths problem, and one of us would say,

"Won't it be great when we can do

what we want, all day, every day!"
And then we'd all sort of daydream about how we were going to spend our summer holidays.

I'm the original 'Action Girl', I'm always on the move, so I imagined us playing rounders and doing lots of other outdoorsy things. I think Fliss fancied having lots of picnics in floaty dresses. P-lease! Lyndz and Rosie didn't seem to care what we did as long as the Sleepover Club did it together. Lyndz likes to get away from her brothers. (Fancy having *four* brothers! Still, I think I'd rather swap with her than have my stupid sister, Molly-the-Monster.) And Rosie just seems to enjoy hanging out with the rest of us.

It's hard to tell what Frankie wanted to do with her holidays. But whatever it was, she'd want to get the rest of us organised to do it too! She doesn't have any brothers and sisters, but you know that already don't you? We all know that because she never stops reminding us about it. She likes doing stuff with the Sleepover Club because she likes having other people to boss around! No, I'm only joking. Frankie's my best friend.

So, anyway, we had all these great plans for our summer holidays and three days into them we were bored. I mean seriously bored. Even a maths lesson followed by a spelling test would have been a treat. The thing is, everything seems to stop for summer. Everybody goes away and everywhere is really quiet.

"Do you think we're the only people in Cuddington who haven't gone away on holiday?" asked Frankie as we were lazing about in the park.

"Yet." said Fliss. "I'm going to…"

"Tenerife. In three weeks." The rest of us said together.

Fliss had told us about her holiday a zillion times already, and we weren't likely to forget.

"I was only saying!" grumbled Fliss and stomped off to the pond to look at the ducks.

"Get her!" laughed Lyndz.

"I wish I was going to Tenerife," moaned Rosie. "I wish I was going *anywhere*. We never go on holiday now."

Frankie, Lyndz and I pretended to play violins. We do that when Rosie is in one of her 'Poor-Little-Me' moods.

"We don't go on holiday much," said Lyndz. "There are too many of us. But I don't mind. There's always lots to do at home."

"But we used to go away a lot. Before dad left," mumbled Rosie. She looked as though she was going to cry. I'm not very good with people who cry. I don't know what to do with them. Lyndz is pretty good, and so is Frankie. I just don't cry very much myself. When I saw Rosie's lip going all wobbly, I thought it was a good time to see what Fliss was up to. She was

11

probably still sulking, but we're used to that by now.

I wanted to see how many cartwheels I could do before I got to the pond where Fliss was standing. I thought it would be about twenty. One, two, three… twelve, thirteen, fourteen…

"Hey, watch it!" I cartwheeled right into Fliss and we both nearly ended up swimming with the ducks!

"Sorry Fliss," I spluttered. My head was in a major spin after being upside down so many times.

"You know Kenny," sighed Fliss, examining her legs for bruises. "You really are very clumsy."

She sounded like Mrs Weaver, our teacher. I wished I'd stayed with the others. Rosie crying would have been better than Fliss moaning.

"*And* I was trying to work something out before you nearly drowned me!" snapped Fliss.

She started muttering something and counting on her fingers. Fliss was certainly one strange dude!

Suddenly, she leapt into the air.

"I thought so. We've had nine! We've had nine!" she shouted.

Yep! That confirmed my original diagnosis – our Fliss had finally flipped!

"Nine what?" I asked. "Nine fights? Nine doughnuts? What?"

Frankie, Lyndz and Rosie had joined us. They had obviously seen the commotion Fliss was causing. What an embarrassment!

"What's she on about?" asked Lyndz. I shrugged my shoulders.

"We've had nine sleepovers!" Fliss shrieked. "That means that the next one will be our tenth!"

"Hey Fliss, go to the top of the class and give the teacher a banana!" I said. "I always knew that you'd learn to count one day!"

"Hang on a minute," said Frankie. "We've had loads of sleepovers. I'm sure we've had more than ten."

"I mean we've had ten since we formed the Sleepover Club with Rosie and everything," explained Fliss very slowly, as though she was talking to a bunch of three-year olds.

"Oh right," Frankie nodded.

"Anyway, as I was saying," continued Fliss. "Ten's an important number, isn't it? We ought to have a special sleepover to celebrate."

Yeah. One-nil! For once, Fliss was right. If we had a sleepover to plan, we couldn't get bored. Especially when it was a special birthday sleepover.

We all felt pretty excited and you know how hyper we can get. We all started talking at once, and laughing and doing high fives as though we'd all just won Olympic medals or something. Somehow I don't think we would have been so enthusiastic if we had known then what trouble this tenth sleepover was going to cause.

The thing is that we're all so different. And I know that that's a good thing, even though it has caused problems in the past. But we always managed to sort them out. And anyway, for our normal sleepovers we just sort of go with the flow, because it's the sleepover that matters and not really what we do there. But for this tenth birthday sleepover, boy did things get out of hand! It was like it wasn't just a sleepover anymore it was some major celebration. We all got very selfish and only wanted to do what *we* wanted to do. Crazy I know. I think we all went a little bit mad for a while.

"We should have a proper party, a dressed-up party, with music and dancing and a proper meal and maybe a marquee and..." said Fliss excitedly.

"What planet are you on Fliss?" I asked. "A marquee? The nearest you'll ever get to a marquee is the tent you sleep in at Brownie camp!"

"Alright Kenny Clever Clogs, what

do you think we should do for the sleepover?" Fliss snapped back. She had those bright-red patches on her cheeks, which is never a good sign.

"What about a day out at one of those paintball courses?"

The others all groaned.

"You only want to do that because you know you'd win. This has to be something special for *all* of us you know." I was surprised when Frankie said that. Us being best mates and everything.

"Alright then, what did you have in mind?" I asked.

"What about a children's party, with silly games and jelly and ice-cream, and balloons…"

"Don't you think we're a bit old for that?" asked Lyndz.

"That's the point," sighed Frankie, coming over all grown-up. "We don't have parties like that anymore because we *think* we're too old, but I think they're kind of fun."

16

"Oh please Frankie," moaned Fliss. "Everybody'd laugh at us if they ever found out!"

"What about going out to the cinema and having a pizza or something," asked Rosie.

"Bor-ing!" the rest of us sang together.

"I was only trying to help!" mumbled Rosie. "I know when I'm not wanted. I might as well go home."

She started walking towards the gate. The rest of us just watched her go. Then we all turned on each other.

"Now see what you've done!"

"What *I've* done. It was *your* fault."

"You always think you know best don't you?"

And before we knew where we were, we were all yelling at each other. And I mean *really* yelling. That's when it looked like the Sleepover Club would never even reach it's tenth birthday!

CHAPTER TWO

So, it was the summer holidays. We were bored. But now the Sleepover Club couldn't even be bored together because we weren't speaking to each other. Crazy hah?

I bet you've done that too haven't you? I mean, I bet you've fallen out with your friends over something really small and stupid. Only it seems really important at the time. It's only later that you realise how dumb the whole thing is. But by then it's too late. The damage is done.

It was awful. I felt totally miserable without the others. But somehow I just couldn't do anything about it. It hadn't been my fault that we'd fallen out in the first place, so why should I be the one to make up? Of course, if we'd all thought like that we would never have spoken to each other again. Frankie and I usually phone each other about a million times a day and we tell each other everything. When we fell out, we didn't speak for three days. Mum is always saying that I can never admit when I'm in the wrong, and I guess that's true.

Looking back it seems stupid that we let everything get so out of hand. But we have our diaries to remind us how awful we felt when we thought the Sleepover Club was about to split up.

I wrote:

If Fliss hadn't thought of having a tenth birthday sleepover party, we'd still all be speaking now. It looks like I'll be stuck with Molly-the-Monster all holidays. Pass the sick bucket! I wish we were going to stay with grandpa and grandma McKenzie now, rather than later in the holidays. At least I wouldn't be bored there. I'm bored bored BORED here without the others.

Frankie wrote in her diary:

Why is it we never agree on anything? If only we could have decided to have a normal party, then none of this would have happened. I don't see what was so wrong with my idea anyway. The others just don't like to do anything different. Well I'm not making the first move to get the Sleepover Club back together. I always end up having to organise everybody. And I'm sick of it.

Fliss wrote in hers:

Went shopping with mum today. She bought me a great pair of shorts and some yellow nail varnish. They're well cool! She said they were to cheer me up, but they haven't. I still miss the others.

Rosie scribbled in her diary:

I'm never going to make any friends again. Nobody likes me. Belonging to the Sleepover Club was great and now

I'm not sure whether there's even going to <u>be</u> one any more. (You couldn't read what else she'd written because the writing was all smudged where she'd cried over it. Breaks your heart doesn't it?)

Lyndz had just written:

Can't stand this anymore. I'm going to ring the others up and get them to meet round here tonight.

And that's just what she did.

It felt a bit weird at first going round to Lyndz's, knowing that there was this big 'thing' between us. We were just so polite with each other. It was as though some crummy old soap opera characters had taken over our bodies and we were sitting around discussing the price of tea or something. It was Frankie who sorted us all out – as usual.

"Look," she said in her grown-up tone of voice. "I'm sorry if I was stroppy the other day. I don't really mind what kind of party we have, as long as we all agree on it." The rest of us mumbled that that was how we felt too. We all looked at the floor, as though our feet were suddenly the most fascinating things in the world.

Suddenly, Lyndz leapt on to her bed and started bouncing on it.

"Come on guys!" she yelled at the top of her voice. "It's party time!" Yep! The Sleepover Club was back together. And just to prove it, Lyndz got hiccups.

"You do realise don't you, that we're the only people in the entire universe who know how to stop you making that appalling noise!" I said, as I dug Lyndz hard in the ribs. A shock like that sometimes does the trick.

"Ouch Kenny!" Lyndz doubled over. "Why do you think I got you all round here? Hic."

"Without us, you'd probably have to walk hiccuping down the aisle on your wedding day," laughed Frankie.

"I, Lyndsey, hic, Marianne, hic,

Collins, hic, do take you, Hic, Hic, Hic..." said Fliss, who knows the whole marriage service backwards.

"Except I'm never getting married," said Lyndsey. "My brothers are enough to put anyone off men for life!" The thought of getting married seemed to have stopped Lyndz's hiccups anyway. Either that or the fact that Frankie had been doing her 'thumb in the hand' routine on her for the last few minutes.

"OK then, so what are we going to do for this party?" asked Frankie when we'd all calmed down. "And where are we going to have it?"

Well, it was like feeding time in the monkey house: we all started chattering at once. And we got louder and louder. And because we were all shouting, nobody could hear what anyone else was saying.

"Shut up!" yelled Frankie. That girl could be a sergeant major with a voice like hers.

"Right," said Frankie, coming over all teacher-like. "If we decide where we're going to have the sleepover, we might be able to decide what we're going to do for it."

"My place would be good," said Fliss. "Because mum's ever so good at organising parties and stuff."

The rest of us weren't very sure about that. Fliss's mum would probably stand over us with a dustpan and brush in case we dropped any fairy cake crumbs on her precious carpet.

"I know my stupid brothers can get in the way," said Lyndz. "But we have got a big garden and my parents are pretty cool about letting us do our own thing."

That was true. But *I* wanted us to have the birthday sleepover at *my* place. That way I could organise a few wild, crazy games and the others couldn't do anything about it. The problem was Molly-the-Monster: the rest of the Sleepover Club dislikes her almost as much as I do – and that's lots!

"It'd be great if we had the sleepover at my place," whispered Rosie. "Adam loves you all coming round. And there are lots of rooms we could use."

Rosie has a stonking great house that her father was supposed to be doing up. He's not around much now, so it's chaotic and a bit run-down. But it's a pretty cool place to hang out. And the staircase is wicked for our 'sliding down the banister' races.

Still, we could have a sleepover there another time. I wanted the tenth birthday one at my place.

"OK, I'm like the rest of you. I'd like you all to come to my place," admitted Frankie. "My room's large, my parents are cool and we've always had pretty great sleepovers there in the past haven't we?"

"Are you saying that the sleepovers

everywhere else weren't much cop?" I asked. "What's wrong with my place?"

"Molly-the-Monster?" Frankie laughed. The others groaned. My stupid sister spoils all my fun.

"How can we decide on where to have it, if we all want it at our own place?" Fliss grumbled. "It's got to be fair!"

"Yeah, yeah, yeah," I moaned. Sometimes I get sick of Fliss going on about what's fair all the time.

"Just because you don't like doing the same things as the rest of us, doesn't mean that you can criticise us all the time," Fliss suddenly turned on me. "And have you ever thought that it might be *you* who's a bit weird for wanting to get all muddy and stinky rather than wearing make-up and having your hair nice?"

Well that was a shock! Fliss wasn't usually so aggressive.

"I'm just not into all that sissy stuff," I said.

"Sissy? That's not fair!" screeched Fliss.

"Fair! Is that all you ever talk about?" I shouted.

And suddenly we were at each other's throats again. This tenth birthday sleepover party looked doomed before the start! But I do admit that this time it was my fault.

"OK. Time out!" shouted Sergeant Major Francesca Thomas. "Have you two any idea what you look like? It's pathetic!"

Fliss and I stopped yelling and looked at each other. Her face was bright red and she looked *mad*! I must have looked like that too, because when we caught sight of each other we just cracked out laughing.

There was a knock at the door.

"I told mum that I'd need danger money to come into a room full of weird women!" Stuart, Lyndz's eldest brother, carried in a tray of orange juice and biscuits.

27

"Come on Lyndz. Shift some of this stuff from your desk. This tray is heavy you know." Lyndz is nearly as untidy as I am. There was so much stuff piled on her desk that when she tried to move it, it fell on to the floor.

"Hey what's this?" asked Rosie, picking something up.

"Oh that's just a card I'm working on for my Artist's Badge at Brownies," said Lyndz taking it from her.

"Oh no! I'd forgotten!" gasped Rosie. "I'll have to start planning it tonight. What else do we have to make? Is it a bookmark?"

"Or a poster," said Fliss.

I hadn't even thought about what I was going to make, and the Badge Tester was coming to Brownies the following Thursday.

"That's it!" shrieked Frankie, grabbing me by the shoulders. "I've done it again! I am a genius!"

"Oi! Let go of me Big Head!" I gasped. "What cunning plan have you thought of now?"

"Well," spluttered Frankie. "We're all doing the Artist's Badge right? If we all design a birthday card for the Sleepover Club, then get the Tester to decide which one is the best, whoever designed the best card gets to hold the tenth birthday sleepover party. I told you I was clever didn't I?"

Frankie was talking so fast that all her words had fallen over each other. So it took the rest of us a little while to work out what she had said. But when we did, we had to admit that the girl's got brains.

Of course, we still had the problem of deciding exactly what we were going to do at this party. But first we were all determined to win the competition.

CHAPTER THREE

After Frankie had had her brainwave we were all eager to get home to design our creative masterpieces. The trouble is that I'm about as good at drawing as an elephant is at roller-skating. If we'd been competing for something like the Athlete's Badge, then I would have started putting up the party streamers. As it was, I knew that I would be going somewhere else for the tenth birthday sleepover party. The question was, where?

My money was on Lyndz winning the competition. She's brilliant at making things. I can sort of see things in my head, but when I try to put my ideas down on paper, they come out all wrong. Lyndz seems to have good ideas, *and* be able to carry them out. Fliss is very prissy and fussy about things. They never quite turn out as she expected them to, but they are always very neat and tidy. And adults always like that don't they?

Frankie is a bit hit-and-miss. Once in art at school, she made this really great dinosaur out of papier-mâché. It was wicked. It stood outside Mrs Poole's office for weeks. Parents would come into school and stand for ages admiring it, like it was by some famous sculptor or something. Then the next time Frankie made a model it was worse than one of those piles of junk you bring home when you're in nursery class. She can be weird like that. You never know what to expect.

I'd never really seen much that Rosie had made. Her last sleepover invitation was pretty neat. But Adam had helped her design it on the computer, so that didn't really count. All I knew for sure was that although I had tried my best with my birthday card, it wasn't going to be good enough to win our competition.

We all met up at Frankie's house a couple of days before Brownies. All the others seemed very confident that their card was going to be the best. But everybody acted like their design was the biggest secret in the universe. Frankie had even asked her father to lock hers away in his filing cabinet. I ask you, how ridiculous can you get?

"If it's a birthday sleepover, are we going to buy presents?" asked Lyndz.

"Oh, we've got to, I love presents!" said Fliss. "This is great. It means we'll all have two birthdays. Like the Queen."

"Hang on one second!" I said, putting on a cheesy American accent. "I mean I love you guys and everything, but I have a serious shortage of dosh. You know what I'm saying?"

"Me too," admitted Rosie. "I never seem to have any money."

Frankie and Lyndz agreed.

A brainwave suddenly hit me:

"Why don't we just give one present each? We don't need to buy it either, we could make it," I said. "I'm sure I could knock something up out of a washing-up bottle and a bit of string. I've seen 'Blue Peter' often enough!"

Who says Frankie should have all the bright ideas?

"I know it's the thought that counts," laughed Lyndz. "But would we really want something you'd made, Kenny?"

The cheek of it! I couldn't let her get away with that. I wrestled her to the ground until she was hiccuping and begging for mercy.

"I'd, hic, love anything you made, hic, Kenny! Really I would!" she spluttered.

"But how would we decide who we were getting the present for?" asked Rosie whilst Frankie dealt with Lyndz's hiccups. She tried a cold marble down her T-shirt for a change. And it worked!

"We could have a lucky dip," said Frankie. "We'll all write our names on a piece of paper, put them in a hat and pull one out. As long as no one picks their own name, it'll be cool."

"And we could keep it a secret. Whose name we've got I mean," said Lyndz. "Then when we get the presents at the party, we'll all have to guess who bought them."

"That means we'll all have to wrap them in the same paper and put them in a special place at the sleepover when nobody else's looking," said Frankie. She always thinks of things like that.

We were all pretty excited about our presents. We each wrote our names on scraps of paper, which Frankie tore out of a notebook. Then she got out her favourite purple velvet hat, and we put all the pieces of paper in it. We each took it in turns to pull out a name. I was the last to pick, so there was only one left. It said:

Fliss

I looked round to try to figure out who had picked my name, but everyone was shoving the papers in their pockets, and had sort of secret smiles on their faces.

"I've seen some great earrings in that shop in the village," said Fliss. "I just thought it might help to give someone a few ideas!"

Oh great! Now we'd have to listen to Fliss dropping hints about her present right up until the sleepover. And we didn't even know when that would be.

"Call me picky…" I said

"Hello Picky!" said the others together.

"Ha! Ha!" I said. "What I was going to

say was, call me picky but it would be nice to know when we're going to have this sleepover. Some of us have lives to plan you know!

"Right! You mean your hectic social life of showbiz premieres and parties I take it!" laughed Frankie.

"I wish!" I said. "I just want to know, that's all."

"Well, I say we should wait until after Brownies on Thursday," said Frankie. "At least then we'll know whose house the sleepover's going to be at. Everything else should be easy to decide after that."

"Right as usual Batman!" I said.

We never usually take this long to plan our sleepovers. I was beginning to think that this one would never happen.

When we saw each other at Brownies on Thursday, we finally showed each other the cards we had been working on for the Artist's Badge. Mine was by far the worst, but that was no surprise. The others were good, but as soon as we saw all our cards together, it was obvious who would be holding the sleepover.

For the Artist's Badge we could design any kind of card. Frankie, Fliss, Lyndz and I had just made ordinary birthday cards. Rosie had made a special *'Happy Tenth Birthday Sleepover Club'* card, complete with a badge.

Coo-ell!
"Wow, Rosie. That's brilliant!" I said.

"You're bound to win! Yours is the best card by miles," said Frankie.

"Thanks very much!" said Fliss.

Frankie ignored her.

"Why don't we just agree that the tenth birthday sleepover will be at Rosie's place?"

Lyndz and I nodded. But Fliss wasn't having that.

"You said that we would ask the Tester to judge the cards," she moaned. "So that's what we should do. She might like something different."

"Like yours you mean?" I asked.

"Maybe," said Fliss.

When we saw who was testing us for our Artist's Badge, we realised why Fliss had been so keen to wait for her opinion. It was Sally Davies, Snowy Owl's best friend. And as I'm sure you remember, Snowy Owl is none other than Fliss's auntie, Jill!

We'd had to do other things for the badge, besides our card. We'd had to design a pattern in three colours and paint or draw a picture. As well as the card, I'd made a bookmark. (I'd painted fluorescent squiggles on it with some of Molly's special paint. She wasn't very happy about that. One-nil!)

Sally looked at all our things separately, then all the Brownies who were taking the badge had to sit at a table together and draw a vase of flowers. I went for the big and colourful look, the others copied what they saw. But that's art isn't it? Everybody looks at things differently.

Sally seemed pleased with everybody's work. She complimented me on my 'bold' style, which sent Frankie into hysterics. When Sally had signed all our forms to say that we had gained the Artist's Badge, Frankie explained about our cards and about the competition we were holding.

"Would you just tell us which card is the best?" she asked.

We'd laid them all out on the table, so it wasn't obvious who had made each one. Although of course she had seen them before and could probably remember.

"I'm not sure that picking out one from the rest is a good idea girls," said Snowy Owl. "You know that everybody's work is as valuable as everybody else's."

We all rolled our eyes to the ceiling.

"No really Auntie Jill, we want Sally to choose," explained Fliss. "We can't decide where to hold our next sleepover, and whoever made the best card gets to hold it at her house. So you see, we really need her help."

Frankie and I nearly cracked up when she said 'Auntie Jill' in that sweet way of hers. She was obviously trying to influence Sally's decision.

"Alright then," said Sally, picking up all the cards and looking at them very carefully. "I think you've all done a fantastic job. But I have to say that this one really stands out because it's so different."

She picked up Rosie's card.

"Putting the badge on there was a very clever idea."

We all patted Rosie on the back. All except Fliss, who scowled at Snowy Owl.

So we finally knew that our tenth birthday sleepover was going to be held at Rosie's house, and that was pretty cool. Not only does she have a humungous house with about a million rooms, but her mum is really great, really young and trendy and a real laugh. The best bit though, is that we can actually write on Rosie's bedroom walls!

I really thought that once we knew where the birthday sleepover was going to be held all our problems were over. How wrong can you be! They were only just beginning!

CHAPTER FOUR

You know the story of Dr Jekyll and Mr Hyde, where the guy has two completely different personalities? Well that was Rosie as soon as she knew that the birthday sleepover was going to be at her place. She was like some power-crazed monster. No one had ever seen her like that before. And I'm certainly not in a hurry to see her like that again.

We all met up at the shops in Cuddington on the Saturday after Brownies. They're easy for us all to get to, apart from Lyndz who lives a little bit further out than the rest of us. And our parents are quite happy for us to go there by ourselves. You know what parents are like! Always worrying about something. But at least they know we're safe there. Apart from the threat of Fliss driving us all crazy by telling us about some great earrings she's just seen, and the cool nail varnish she 'just has to have'. P-lease!

We always meet on the same bench outside the newsagents. Rosie was the last to arrive. When she did appear, she was carrying a mountain of paper.

"What on earth have you got there?" asked Lyndz.

"Plans for the sleepover. Is next Saturday alright?" asked Rosie, flopping down next to us.

"Now, let me just consult my diary," I said, pretending to flick through some imaginary pages. "Let me see. Next Saturday you say? Hmm. I think I can squeeze you in!"

"Sounds good to me!" said Lyndz.

"Fine by me," agreed Frankie.

"So we've got a week to sort the presents out!" said Fliss. The rest of us groaned.

From the pile she was carrying, Rosie pulled out four invitations. Pinned to each one was a copy of the badge she'd made for Brownies.

Rosie invites you to the special

10th

BIRTHDAY SLEEPOVER
at
75 Welby Drive
Welby Avenue
Cuddington Leicester

Please come at 5pm on
Saturday 27th July
Be prepared to
PARTY!

"Cool!" we all gasped.

"Adam did these on the computer for me. I thought it would be nice if we could all wear one for the sleepover," she seemed very pleased with herself. "All you've got to do is cut them out and make them into a badge. Is that OK?"

"Yep, I think even we can manage that!" I laughed, pulling a face at Frankie.

"Now," said Rosie, reading from one of her larger sheets of paper. "What I thought was: arrive at 5pm, put things in my room until 5.15pm, games outside until 6.15pm, make-up and hair, (possibly a fashion show if we can fit it in) until 7pm, food until 7.45pm, Twister until 8.15pm, then disco until mum sends us to bed, which she says will be about 10pm – if we're lucky! Washing and undressing until 10.30pm, giving out presents until 11pm, then midnight feast. Everybody OK with that?"

We were all sitting round with our jaws scraping the pavement. Was this girl for real? This was more like a military exercise than a sleepover. It was supposed to be *fun* for goodness sake!

"Erm, Rosie, I think you've forgotten one thing," I said very seriously.

"No, I can't have. I was up all night planning this. What have I forgotten?" she said, furiously reading through her timetable.

"What about toilet breaks?" I giggled. "I mean what if we need to go to the loo in the middle of the outdoor games? Should you plan for us to all to go together just to be on the safe side? Then we won't mess up your timetable."

"Like at school you mean?" Rosie looked very thoughtful. "That's not a bad idea. I'll see where I can fit it in." The rest of us cracked up. Even Fliss knew that I was joking and Fliss has a sense of humour the size of a pea.

"And I'm not sure about the beginning bit," said Lyndz. Rosie flicked through her notes. "You mean 'arrive at 5pm put things in my room at 5.15pm?' What's wrong with that?"

"Well what if one of us is late? Or it takes us longer to get our stuff sorted out?" asked Lyndz.

"Yes and where are we going to put the presents so the others can't see them?" asked Fliss.

"Oh no!" gasped Rosie. "I've got to do some more planning. But you can't be late. You just can't be. It'll mess everything up if you are!" She looked as though she was going to cry.

"Don't you think you're taking this a bit seriously?" asked Frankie gently.

"I just want it all to be perfect, what's wrong with that?" snapped Rosie. "It's not just any old sleepover. It's our tenth birthday sleepover and I want to make sure we'll all remember it."

She was certainly right about that. I don't think any of us will ever forget it!

"Is there anything you want us to bring?" I asked. "Stopwatches, so we don't run over time? Running shoes so we can sprint from one thing to another?"

"Party clothes? Balloons? Cuddly toy?" asked Frankie.

"What about the cake?" asked Fliss. "We've got to have a cake."

Rosie began to search frantically through all her sheets of paper.

"The cake!" she shrieked. "How could I forget about the cake?"

It was a bit sad really, seeing her get so upset.

"Don't worry. We could buy one," I suggested.

"We've no money," Lyndz reminded me.

"Well let's make one then!" Frankie said.

Now the Sleepover Club are not exactly the greatest bakers in the world. In fact, we are a total disaster in the kitchen.

"Is that a good idea?" asked Fliss. Her mum never lets her loose in their gleaming white kitchen. Not after we nearly burnt the place down anyway.

"Sure it is!" said Lyndz very confidently. "My mum's a mean cook. She'll give us a hand. She likes getting the chance to do stuff like that. She's always complaining that my brothers aren't interested in anything domestic. And neither am I, usually."

"We'll have to do it before next Saturday," Rosie reminded her. "Is that OK?"

"No probs," said Lyndz. "I'll ask mum when I get back this afternoon and give you a ring. You can all come over to my place and we'll have a girlie afternoon in the kitchen!"

Now I don't know about you, but cooking isn't really my thing. Eating, yes. Cooking, no way. But what could I do? I couldn't let my friends down now, could I? So when Lyndz rang that evening to say that we could all go there on the Friday before the sleepover to bake the cake, well how could I refuse?

Anyway, before that I had other things on my mind – like what to give Fliss for her stupid sleepover birthday present!

I know that this sounds really mean, but I really resented having to spend my pocket money on something which Fliss would like for five minutes and then throw away. She's like that is Fliss. She has to have all the latest fashions she sees in magazines, then when the next thing comes along, she forgets how desperate she was for this skirt, or that pair of trainers, and she wants something else. Frankie reckons that I'm jealous, but it's not that. I'll be quite happy wearing my Leicester City football shirt until I die. I don't like frills and sequins like Fliss. And I don't really care how I look.

I know it sounds really petty, but I didn't want to buy her the earrings that she liked, just because she'd hinted that she wanted them. That would have felt like she'd won. I was determined to give her something different. And I wanted to make it myself, just to prove that I could.

I rummaged about under my bed. I was bound to find something useful there. I found piles of old football magazines, a couple of stinky socks which didn't match, a baby's dummy (I have no idea where that came from) and a length of clear plastic tubing. I couldn't remember where I'd found the tubing, it was just something that I thought might come in useful one day!

I didn't think Fliss would be very impressed by hand puppets made out of the socks. And I wasn't going to sacrifice my football magazines for anybody. I picked up the tubing. It was so long that I could use it as a skipping rope. It was ages since I'd skipped. It was pretty cool!

"Watch it! You'll go through the floor!" snarled Molly-the-Monster as she came into the room. "What is that anyway?"

"Plastic tubing," I said showing it to her.

She wrapped it around her waist, then draped it around her neck.

"What do you want it for?" she asked, looking at herself in the mirror.

"Dunno. Something," I shrugged.

"If you decide you don't want it, I'll have it," she said, and slammed the door behind her as she went out.

That settled it. If Molly thought that the tubing was worth having, then I was going to keep it for Fliss's present.

I still wasn't sure what I was going to do with it though. I had some glitter left from the card I'd made for my Artist's Badge. I held the tubing so there was only a short length, and poured some glitter into it. It looked brilliant, even if I say so myself. It was exactly the kind of thing that Fliss loves. So that's when I decided to make her some glittery bracelets for her present.

When I had finished, I was well pleased with my efforts. Even Fliss should be kind of impressed. And no way would she ever suspect me of making the bracelets.

So then 'there was a long boring week until the Friday when we all met up again at Lyndz's for the great birthday cake bake. And what an event *that* turned out to be.

CHAPTER FIVE

If I'm honest, I wasn't looking forward to the cooking party at Lyndz's. I enjoy being with the others and everything. And Lyndz's mum is great. It's just *cooking*! You know what I'm saying?

Frankie had organised which cake ingredients we should each take to Lyndz's. I had the huge responsibility of providing the flour.

"You do know that it's self-raising flour we need, don't you Kenny?" Frankie asked over the phone.

"You mean it can lift itself off the

shelf, all by itself?" I asked really innocently.

"You are joking, right?" she asked.

"Of course I am, dummy!" I laughed. "I may not be into baking, but I think I know what kind of flour we need for a cake!"

So, on Friday afternoon, I arrived at Lyndz's armed with a bag of flour. I thought that at least if things got really bad, I could make flour bombs with it. Although I don't think Lyndz's mum would have been too thrilled about that.

I was the last to arrive. The others were already in the kitchen with their hair tied back and their pinnies on. Aw, sweet!

"Here she is! Our vital ingredient!" laughed Lyndz's mum when she saw me.

"That's me!" I said. "You can't do anything without Laura McKenzie!"

I put the bag of flour down on the work surface next to the butter, the sugar, the icing sugar and the eggs.

"Have you got an apron?" Lyndz's mum asked me. The others spluttered with laughter.

"Kenny? Wearing an apron? You must be joking!"

"I hope you don't spoil your football shirt," said Lyndz's mum seriously.

"How can she spoil it when it already looks like an old dishcloth?" asked Frankie. I strutted around the kitchen as though I was modelling an expensive ball-gown in a fashion show.

Then the others went into Delia Smith mode. (I'm not going to bore you with all the details. Baking a cake isn't the most exciting thing in the world. I'll just give you 'Kenny's edited highlights' of the afternoon, which is all you really need to know.)

After the others had weighed out the butter and sugar and put them into a bowl, Lyndz asked her mum if we could use the electric whisk.

"Yes, but be careful. Are your hands

dry?" She felt all our hands. "OK. Turn it on at the mains, then turn the whisk on gently to start with and keep the beaters in the bowl. Whilst one of you does that, someone else can be breaking those two eggs into a bowl. Careful not to let any shells in. When you've done that give them a good whizz together with a fork. Now that's you lot sorted, you haven't seen Spike anywhere have you?"

Spike is Lyndz's baby brother. I think even I would have noticed if a baby had been crawling around the kitchen floor.

"Let me have a go! Please can I use the whisk?" begged Fliss.

"What are you like Fliss?" asked Frankie. "Is using an electric whisk the biggest thrill of your life?"

Fliss does tend to get a bit excited about weird stuff like whisks!

"This is cool!" she laughed.

Lyndz's mum disappeared again on the track of Spike. It's usually quite easy to find him: you just follow the trail of biscuit crumbs.

I was getting a bit bored. Fliss looked very serious. The temptation was too much. I sneaked up behind her and, yelling "Gotcha!", I tickled her under the arms. Fliss jumped a mile and forgot that she was holding the whisk. She lifted it out of the bowl and mixture flew everywhere.

"Turn it off!" yelled Frankie, who almost dropped the bowl of eggs she was beating.

"I can't!" shouted Fliss who seemed to have completely lost control.

The whisk suddenly stopped whizzing. Lyndz had turned it off at the mains.

"You stupid idiot!" yelled Fliss, turning on me.

"I'm sorry," I said. "I didn't know that was going to happen."

We looked round the kitchen. Everything was covered in tiny splatters of creamed sugar and butter.

"We ought to try and clean some of this up before your mum comes back," said Frankie. She grabbed a dishcloth and started to wipe up the worst of the mess. The rest of us grabbed kitchen roll and started to do the same. I couldn't help grinning to myself: an electric whisk was a pretty cool weapon.

By the time Lyndz's mum re-appeared, the worst of the mess was gone and the others were dropping tiny bits of egg into the mixture and giving it a good stir. Yawn, yawn, how boring!

Next we sieved the flour. I hadn't helped with the baking at all so Frankie made *me* hold the sieve. She said that even I couldn't get that wrong. And it really wasn't my fault when I covered everyone in flour. It was Spike's! He charged right into me and the sieve flew out of my hand. It was like a snowstorm! Fortunately Lyndz's mum knew it wasn't my fault.

But that didn't stop the others from having a go at me – especially Fliss. Her hair was covered in flour. She looked like someone's granny!

"If you're not doing anything Kenny," said Frankie, "you might as well make a start on the washing-up!" Charming!

"Right sir!" I shouted like a soldier and saluted to her. Frankie grinned.

I was up to my elbows in dirty dishes and bubbles when Lyndz's brother Ben appeared. I didn't see him dropping pieces of Lego into the cake mixture. I didn't see him trying to feed it to Buster, the dog. But I did feel it on the back of my neck when he threw a handful at me.

"Oi! What are you doing you horror?" I shouted.

The others were already yelling and fishing the Lego out of the cake. They were not happy bunnies.

"Go to Mum!" Lyndz shouted. Even *she* can lose her cool sometimes.

The last thing we had to do was pour the mixture into the two tins. That was not as easy as it sounds, but we managed it in the end. And Buster ate all the dollops that fell onto the floor, so they didn't really matter.

"Mum! We're ready to put them into the oven now!" yelled Lyndz. She's another who could be a sergeant major!

Stuart appeared.

"Mum says I've to put them into the oven for you," he said. He stuck his finger into one of the tins. "Hmm. Not bad!"

"Aw Stuart!" moaned Lyndz. "We took ages smoothing the top of that. Now we'll have to do it again."

"Well hurry up," grumbled her brother. "I've got to leave for the farm in a minute."

"Be careful they don't mistake you for one of the pigs, won't you!" laughed Lyndz.

"Ha, ha!" said Stuart. "Do you want

these in the oven or not?" He took the tins from Lyndz and put them on the middle shelf in the oven.

"Save me a bit of cake won't you?" he called as he left. "I did play a vital role in making it!"

We ignored him.

"The recipe book says '25–30 minutes cooking time'," read out Lyndz. "Who can remember that? What time is it now?" Lyndz is hopeless at telling the time, so we all looked at our own watches.

"Ten past four," we all said together.

"So we should look at the cake at twenty-five to five then," said Frankie.

Lyndz looked very confused, but the rest of us agreed.

When we'd finished the rest of the washing-up and had cleared away, we messed about with Spike and Ben. Then we went out into the garden.

"How's your cake doing?" Mrs Collins called out to us. We all looked at each other. The cake! We'd forgotten all about it! It was almost ten to five. We raced inside. The kitchen was filled with sort of a thick, not quite a burnt smell.

"Quick! Mum! We'll have to get the cakes out now!" yelled Lyndz.

"Don't panic!" laughed her mum, opening the oven door. "There now. They look great!"

They didn't look great exactly. But they didn't look too bad. And when they'd cooled and we'd sandwiched them together with jam and put icing on top, the birthday cake looked all right.

We all shared the icing bit. It read:

Happy Birthday
Sleepover Club

Now we were all set for the party.

CHAPTER SIX

I woke up really early on Saturday morning. It wasn't just excitement that woke me, it was something else as well – rain. It was pouring down. Not only that, but it was windy too. I couldn't believe it! Until then every day had been warm and sunny. Now it felt more like November than the middle of July! Miserable or what?

"Your stupid sleepover party's going to be a bit of a washout. What a pity!" laughed Molly-the-Monster peeping out from her duvet.

"Shut up!" I yelled and hit her with

my pillow. She's only jealous because I go to more sleepovers than she does.

"Ouch! That hurt!" she screamed and thwacked me with her own pillow. "At least I'll be able to get some peace and quiet in my *own* room tonight."

I wish that we lived in a house like Rosie's, then I could have my own bedroom. I hate sharing a room with Monster Features.

The rain didn't stop all day. I kept looking out of the window to check. By 4.30pm it was raining so heavily that I expected to see Noah floating past the house in his ark!

"Looks like you're going to have a wet one, love!" said Mum as I climbed into her car. "You have packed enough warm things, haven't you?"

"Yes Mum!" I sighed, as I pinned on my 'Happy Tenth Birthday Sleepover Club' badge. She'd asked me that about a thousand times already.

We usually walk to sleepovers, especially in the summer. We don't live very far from each other, as you know. But seeing as it was so wet, mum had arranged to give Frankie a lift to Rosie's. Lyndz and Fliss were going together.

"Poor Rosie," said Frankie as she got into the car. "I bet she hadn't planned for rain."

"Oh, I don't know," I said. " Now the timetable probably says 'Come in and drip in the hallway until 5.01pm, remove raincoats until 5.02pm, then water sports in the garden until 5.37 precisely'."

Frankie and I both giggled.

"I hope you're not being unkind, Laura McKenzie," said Mum. "I think Rosie sounds like a very organised young lady, and it wouldn't do you any harm to take a leaf out of her book!"

"Aw, Mum!" I groaned. "It's so boring!"

We pulled up outside Rosie's house. Two pathetic balloons were dangling from the gate. They made me feel a bit sad.

"Oh no!" gasped Frankie. "It's 5.02pm. We're late!" I put my hand to my forehead in mock despair.

"Oh no! How could we be so irresponsible?" I cried. "Rosie will never forgive us!"

"Now girls," warned mum quite sternly. "Don't go upsetting Rosie. Oh look, here come Lyndz and Fliss."

Lyndz's dad drew up in his large van and Lyndz and Fliss leapt out.

"We're late!" they both shouted and we all laughed. We were all wearing our special badges and we felt pretty cool.

We started walking up the path and a huge gust of wind hit us. It lifted Fliss so far off the ground that she looked as though she was flying!

"I always knew you were a witch Fliss!" I laughed.

"You're too skinny," said Lyndz digging her in the ribs. "You need building up."

Fliss looked a bit flustered, then

kept saying, "Did you see me fly? I actually got right off the ground. Did you see?"

Frankie and I looked at each other and rolled our eyes. We would *never* hear the end of it now!

When we got to Rosie's front door, there was a soggy piece of paper stuck to it. It said 'TIMETABLE' in smudged ink. The first item – 'Outdoor Games' – had been crossed out.

"Oh dear!" muttered Frankie.

Rosie came to the door, even before we'd knocked.

"Sorry we're late," we all said together.

"Doesn't matter," mumbled Rosie. "You'd better come in."

It was almost as gloomy inside the house as it was outside.

"Hi Adam!" I called, seeing Rosie's brother in the hall. He just nodded. You remember Adam don't you? He's got cerebral palsy, and is in a wheelchair. He's got a wicked sense of humour and he's usually heaps of fun. Not on Saturday he wasn't. He just sulked in a corner and looked miserable.

"What's up with him?" I asked Rosie as we went up to her bedroom.

"Dad promised to take him fishing, but he had to cancel. He had a big job to finish or something." Rosie sounded miserable too.

We all looked anxiously at each other behind Rosie's back. Somehow this wasn't turning out to be the fun birthday party we'd expected.

"Where shall we put our presents?" asked Fliss.

"There's a big sack in the room next to the bathroom. I've put mine in it already. If the rest of you put yours in, mum said I could lock the door and then get the presents out again at bedtime," explained Rosie.

"Cool!"

We'd all arranged to wrap our presents in brown paper so that they would all look similar. We sneaked out of Rosie's bedroom separately and put the presents in the sack. When it was my turn I had a feel at the ones that were already in there. They all felt very interesting, but I couldn't tell what anything was. I couldn't find mine either!

When we had all put our presents in the sack, Rosie locked the door and put the key under her pillow.

"Right then Batman. What have you got planned instead of outdoor games?" I asked Rosie.

"Well, I haven't really," she muttered.

"What! Nothing planned?" I shrieked. "That's outrageous! We expect better of you Miss Cartwright! Don't we girls!" The others looked very serious and nodded.

Rosie began to smile.

"Well I thought maybe we could play 'Hide and Seek'," she said quietly. "If that's alright with you."

"Cool!"

"Wicked!"

"Brill!"

Rosie looked happy again. Then Tiffany, her sister, burst into the room.

"I hope you lot aren't going to be noisy all afternoon!" she snapped.

Noisy? That wasn't noisy! She hadn't heard anything yet! Her boyfriend, Spud, appeared in the doorway behind her.

"Aw Tiff, give them a break," he said. "Let them have a laugh."

Still scowling, she walked downstairs after him.

"What's her problem?" asked Frankie.

"Mum's had to go somewhere for one of her assignments at college. And she's left Tiff and Spud in charge until she gets back. Tiff is not very pleased!" explained Rosie. She looked as though she was going to get miserable again, so I said,

"I'll be 'it'. 1,2,3,..."

The others screamed and I could hear them scampering away to hide.

"...99,100. Coming! Ready or not!"

Rosie's house is a pretty cool house to hide in – but not such a great place to do the seeking in! There seem to be so many secret places that you just couldn't possibly know about. Usually Adam is a great help to whoever is seeking. He kind of gestures with his head, and creeps up behind you silently in his wheelchair and moves to where someone is hiding.

"Any clues Adam?" I called to him when I passed him in the hallway. But he just sat there looking sad. Surely Rosie's father's job couldn't have been that important. If Adam were my son, I'd always take him fishing when I promised him that I would.

"Hic!"

Lyndz is always easy to find. The excitement gets to her, then she starts hiccuping.

"Easy-peasy!" I told her. Then she giggled even more and went bright red.

"Honestly Lyndz. What are you

like!" I laughed. "Come on. Help me find the others."

We eventually found Frankie in a cloakroom downstairs. She was under a pile of coats and it was only her big feet that gave her away! I would recognise those trainers anywhere! Rosie was harder to find, but that's not surprising when it's her house and she knows all its secret places. There's a staircase, which leads to more rooms in the roof, and sort of tucked underneath it is a tiny hiding space. We only found it by accident because Lyndz tripped over and fell into it.

"Ouch!" cried a voice. We'd found Rosie!

After another half an hour of looking we still hadn't found Fliss. And we were bored. We shouted that we were giving up the search.

"Do you suppose she's heard us?" asked Rosie.

"'Course she has!" I said. "She just wants to make us sweat. Let's go and play something else. She'll come to us when she's fed up!"

"What time is it anyway?" asked Lyndz.

"Time you learnt to tell the time yourself!" Frankie and I shouted together.

"It's just after six," said Rosie. "That means it's almost time for doing makeovers."

"Can't we play something else first?" I pleaded. Hopefully, we'd get so involved in another game, the others would forget about the stupid makeovers.

"Let's play 'Tell Me'," said Rosie. "I've set it up in the lounge, just in case."

"Crikey Rosie. You've thought of everything haven't you?" said Frankie. You could see she was impressed. After that, Rosie's face was just one huge grin. If Frankie was impressed by her organisation, she was on to a winner!

We were in full flow with 'Tell Me',

yelling and shouting at each other, when the door opened. In came Fliss. Boy, did she look angry!

"Where've *you* been then?" I asked her as I spun the wheel.

"Hiding. I thought we were playing 'Hide and Seek'. I must have been wrong." Her mouth was set in a thin, tight line and she spat the words out.

"Keep your hair on!" I said. "Didn't you hear us calling to tell you that we gave up. Where were you hiding anyway?"

"In a cupboard in the bathroom. And it was very hot and very spooky in there by myself!"

"Come and sit down, Fliss. You can play with me if you want," said Rosie.

"I thought *you* might have waited for me," Fliss turned on Rosie. Rosie's smile disappeared again. She looked sadder than ever. The rest of us gave Fliss some of our 'black looks'. It had taken us ages to cheer Rosie up, trust Fliss to spoil it.

"What?" asked Fliss. "Why are you all looking at me like that?"

"Because..."

But we couldn't finish because an enormous CRASH shook the room and we all started to scream.

CHAPTER SEVEN

While we were screaming, two things seemed to happen together: firstly, we noticed that the large window in the lounge had shattered, and secondly, Rosie's mother appeared.

"Mum! What have you done?" Rosie wailed. She was staring at her mother as though she had just made her entrance by leaping through the window.

"Darling are you alright?" asked Mrs Cartwright. "Are you all alright? You haven't been cut by flying glass have you? Are you sure?" She was looking at us all anxiously.

"Why did you do that?" asked Rosie. She was still in a state of shock.

"Do what?" asked Rosie's mum. "I was just coming in the front door when there was an enormous gust of wind. I heard it shattering the window and I came in here. I didn't realise that you were here. Are you sure that you're alright?"

She looked at us carefully, checking for cuts. I was all prepared with my First Aid if anyone needed any assistance. Unfortunately they didn't.

"Did the wind make you fly?" asked Fliss. "It made me fly, didn't it Frankie?" Frankie sighed and nodded.

"No, I'm afraid I didn't fly Fliss," said Rosie's mum. "But that certainly sounds like fun." Fliss smiled and nodded. Rosie began to cry.

"Oh-oh," I muttered under my breath.

"What's the matter darling?" asked her mum, putting an arm around

Rosie's shaking shoulders.

"It's not fair!" cried Rosie. "Why does everything always go wrong for me? I wanted this sleepover to be perfect. I bet it wouldn't even have rained if it had been at someone else's house. But whenever *I* do anything, it always goes wrong."

"Don't be silly darling," said her mum. "It would have been raining today, wherever the sleepover had been."

"Yes and we wouldn't have had such a great time playing 'Hide and Seek' at anyone else's house," said Lyndz. "Your house is best for that."

Fliss tutted. She still hadn't forgiven us for leaving her, and something told me it would be a long time before she did.

"Yes, but what about the window?" said Rosie. "I bet that wouldn't have happened at one of your houses."

"That could have happened anywhere with this wind," Mrs

Cartwright reassured her. "It's just that our house is quite old, and some of the windows need replacing."

Rosie lost it completely when she said that.

"It's not fair. S'not fair," she sobbed. It was awful. I felt bad for Rosie and everything. But I couldn't see what the big deal was. I'd love it if a window smashed in our lounge. Nothing like that ever happens at my house.

Tiff and Spud appeared with brushes and newspaper and bin liners.

"Thanks you two," said Mrs Cartwright. "You can sweep the glass into a pile, but leave it for me to pick up."

Tiff sighed and stomped off with the brush.

"I'm just going to phone your father to see if he'll come round and board up the window..." continued Rosie's mum. Rosie let out another howl. "...You girls go upstairs to Rosie's room," said Mrs Cartwright, shooing us through the door, "and I'll call you when your food's ready."

We all trooped off upstairs. Frankie and Lyndz had their arms around Rosie. Fliss was pretending to fly up the stairs. And I was thinking what a crummy party this was turning out to be. It wasn't Rosie's fault, it was just that everyone seemed so *wet* sometimes. What we needed was a good old Gladiator fight or something. But when I suggested it Frankie went ballistic.

"Kenny, for goodness sake! Can't you see how upset Rosie is? I don't think bashing each other about is exactly what she needs right now!" she said.

So much for that idea. I knew that I could do with bashing someone about to make me feel better.

It was pretty gloomy in Rosie's room. We had to turn on the light even though it wasn't very late. The dark sky and rain outside made it feel like

November again.

I hate it when everyone is really quiet. I felt that I should say something to break the silence.

"The way that window smashed! It was way cool!" I said. The others shot me a look.

"Kenny!" warned Frankie. "Shut up can't you?"

"Sorry for breathing!" I snapped back. What was wrong with everybody?

"It's going to look like a squat isn't it?" mumbled Rosie through her tears.

"What do you mean?" asked Lyndz.

"With the window boarded up. Everybody's going to think that I live in some run-down shack," Rosie wailed.

"Don't be silly!" I said. "It'll only be for one night, then someone can replace the window tomorrow, or Monday at the latest. No one's even going to notice it." Rosie stopped crying.

"Actually Rosie, you look pretty awful," I laughed. "We'll have to do something about those red eyes. It's just not a good look for you, darling!" The others laughed too.

"Come on then Fliss. Do your stuff with that make-up!" I said.

"Are you having make-up on as well?" asked Rosie.

I could feel the others all staring at me. Now you know me and make-up. Yeuch! is all I can say. But this was an exception, and I only did it for Rosie because she was so upset. I'll admit it: for the first – and last – time, I let Fliss make me up. The others were more bothered about that than having their own make-up done. And usually they all argue about who should have theirs done first and which eye shadow they should wear. On the birthday Saturday, they stood about watching me with their chins scraping the floor. I mean p-lease! Anyone would think I was some rare animal in a zoo or something.

"So, how do I look?" I asked pouting

and posing like a model.

"Wicked!"

"Coo-el!"

"You really ought to wear it more often. It really suits you," said Fliss standing back to admire her handiwork.

"Ta very much!" I shrieked, pretending to be upset. "Are you saying that I'm ugly the rest of the time?"

"Well yes actually, we are!" Frankie laughed.

I grabbed her by the arms and wrestled her to the floor. That was more like it! Everyone seemed to be having fun, piling on top of us and shrieking. It was almost worth the embarrassment of wearing blue eyeshadow and pink lipstick to have everyone back to normal again. But I knew that it was too good to last. The light suddenly flickered, then it went out completely.

We were all in a pile on the floor and

I was at the bottom. So I thought I was going to get squashed when Fliss started screaming and didn't move. What is it about lights going out that makes people scream? I mean, what did she really think was going to happen? Did she honestly think that there was some monster lurking about who had turned out the lights so it could come in and eat us all up? I don't think so.

"Fliss! Shut up and get up!" I gasped.

By that time Rosie had started screaming too. Thank goodness Frankie is a bit more together. She forced her way out of the pile of bodies and stumbled to the window. We could see that it was completely dark outside – no street lights, nothing.

"It's OK," she said. "Nobody's got any lights on. There must have been a power cut!"

We all crowded round the window to have a look out. It's funny isn't it?

You think you know somewhere really well, but when you look at it differently, like when there are no lights on, it's like you're seeing it for the first time. Rosie's front garden looked massive. And because it had been raining so hard, it looked as though there was a stream running down the middle of it.

"This is wicked!" I said.

"It's a bit spooky!" said Fliss, shivering.

The door creaked open. We all jumped about a mile. All we could see at first was a light shining towards us.

"Are you alright girls?" It was Mrs Cartwright. "It's only a power cut. Have you brought your torches? I could only find this one."

We always take our torches to sleepovers. We scrambled about in our sleeping bags and found them.

"Do you want to come downstairs and stay with us until your food's ready?" asked Rosie's mum.

"No thanks Mum. We'll be fine up here," said Rosie.

"OK I'll call you. It won't be long," said her mum and closed the door behind her.

"Rosie, this is so cool!" Lyndz squeaked, hugging Rosie.

You could tell that Rosie wished she'd planned the whole thing herself. At last the tenth birthday sleepover was turning into a party worth remembering!

CHAPTER EIGHT

Rosie has this big double bed in her bedroom. But then you probably remember that, right? Well, it was really cool, because we could all sit on it and spook each other out. We held the torches under our chins and pulled gruesome faces. Fliss kept screaming and hiding her face in Rosie's shoulder. What is she like?

Then we started to tell ghost stories and that *really* scared Fliss. She kept screaming "Shut up! Please shut up!" But of course the more she did that, the more we thought of even spookier stories. Frankie's brill at all that stuff, but she knows she is and acts really cool about it.

"There was once a haunted house, very much like Rosie's house actually," she started. Nobody moved. "It had lots of rooms, it had cellars and attics, very much like here. And under the attic stairs there was a secret passage that no one knew about. Except the ghost!"

We all squealed a bit and huddled closer together.

"It was the ghost of a man who used to live in the house. It was the only place he'd ever been happy. So he slid through the walls and watched over the family who lived there now. They never saw the ghost, they just felt an icy chill whenever he came into the room."

We huddled closer together still, so that we could almost feel each other breathing.

"One day the girl of the house, who

was very much like Rosie, was in her bedroom with some of her friends when…"

Rosie's bedroom door squeaked open and a rush of cold air filled the room. We all screamed with fright. We clung to each other and kept our heads down. If that was the ghost, we didn't want to see him.

"Well, I know I'm irresistible girls, but I didn't know I was *that* irresistible!" It was only Spud. "Your mum asked me to tell you that 'grub's up'!"

I could feel my heart booming inside my chest. I didn't think it would ever get back to normal.

"That was chilling, Frankie!" I told her.

"How did you arrange with Spud to come in at just the right moment?" asked Fliss. You could tell she was still shaken, but she was desperate not to let the rest of us see.

"Well, you know Fliss, I didn't,"

Frankie said very seriously. "I reckon the ghost must have told him when to come in!"

"Aaah! Frankie don't say that!" Fliss seemed to have gone very pale, although it was hard to tell by torchlight.

We all trooped downstairs, stumbling a bit as we went. Tiffany was at the bottom of the stairs, shining a torch to show us the way into the dining room.

"Hey Tiff, you could get a job in the cinema," laughed Rosie.

"Shut your face!" said her sister, but even she looked happier than she had done earlier.

Eating is one of my favourite things, after Leicester City of course, and I was getting very hungry. It seemed like the others were too, because we all barged into each other and bundled into the dining room. We couldn't believe what we saw there. It was mega-wicked. Everywhere was glowing with candlelight. There were loads of candles in jam jars down the middle of the table and on the fireplace. There were even a couple of lanterns hanging in the window.

"Oh wow!" said Rosie. "This is brilliant, Mum!"

The rest of us gasped and just stood there gawping. It was like we couldn't even move.

"I know that I don't need to tell you this, because I know that you're all sensible girls," said Mrs Cartwright. "But candles are dangerous, so I don't want you touching them. OK? Right, lecture over. Who's for pizza!"

"Me!" we all shouted and made a dive for the table.

In the other room we could hear voices. One was Spud's.

"Is Dad here?" Rosie called to her mum.

"Yes, he's just doing the window. Spud and Adam are helping him," she called back.

"I'd forgotten about that," said Rosie glumly.

"Don't worry," I told her. "It's so dark we won't even be able to see it."

"I suppose not," she said, but she'd gone all sad again.

"Oh come on Rosie, cheer up!" said Frankie. "This is one of the best parties I've ever been to. And it hasn't really started yet! What's next on your timetable?"

Rosie pulled out a scruffy bit of paper from her pocket. She held it up to one of the lanterns on the table.

"Oh no!" she yelled, slamming her fist down. "I didn't think anything else could go wrong!"

"What's up?" I asked. "Don't tell me we've run over time with the meal! We haven't even had the cake yet!"

"Nope. It's worse than that," sighed Rosie shoving the paper back in her pocket. "I'd got everything ready for a disco..."

"We can dance by candlelight. It'll

be cool!" shouted Lyndz.

"There's just one little problem," mumbled Rosie.

"What?" we all asked.

"No power. How can we play my cassettes if we've no electricity?"

She was right. That certainly was a problem.

"How come your mum's cooked the pizza and garlic bread if there's still a power cut?" asked Fliss.

"We've got a gas cooker Fliss," said Mrs Cartwright who had just come in to collect our plates.

"Mum..." Rosie called, but she'd gone out of the room again.

"We could play Twister by candlelight," suggested Frankie. "It'll be a laugh."

"I suppose we'll have to," said Rosie. "Unless anybody can think of something else we can do instead."

"I know!" I shouted. "Let's have the birthday cake! Seeing as I helped to make it!"

"You?" shouted the others.

"I don't think holding a sieve actually counts as 'helping' does it?" asked Frankie. I was suddenly bombarded by handfuls of crisps and popcorn. Charming! So that's all the thanks I get for losing my cred in the kitchen!

"Oi! Watch it you lot!" shouted Tiffany.

We looked up. She had just come into the room and was carrying our cake. Ten candles were flickering on top of it. It was class! I know we'd all seen birthday cakes before, but this was really special. It might have been because we'd made the cake ourselves. Or it might have been because the room looked pretty cool anyway with all the other candles. Whatever it was, for a few moments none of us could speak. Then we all sort of squealed together. I know that it sounds a bit nerdy now. I guess you just had to be there.

"We've all got to blow the candles out together and make a wish," said Fliss.

So we sang *'Happy birthday to us, Happy Birthday to us, Happy Birthday dear Sleepover Club, Happy Birthday to us!'*, then we all took an enormous breath and whoosh! All the candles were blown out. I can't tell you what I wished for, obviously, or else it won't come true. But you can have a guess.

As far as the actual cake was concerned, well, I'd be lying to you if I said it was the best cake I'd ever tasted. But it wasn't too bad. None of us went down with food poisoning anyway.

When we'd all finished, Rosie said "Right then, we might as well go into the lounge and play Twister."

Tiff, who was clearing up the table, shouted "No! Not yet!" just like that. It was really weird.

"Why not?" asked Rosie, sounding a bit miffed.

"Because..." spluttered her sister.

"Because Tiffany's been helping me all evening and she thought that you could all help to clear the table," explained Rosie's mum.

We didn't mind doing that, and she was right, Tiff had been helping out with the food and everything. I'm sure that she would rather have been out with Spud somewhere. She hadn't even grumbled about it either.

While we were taking the plates and stuff into the kitchen, Rosie's mum went into the lounge. We could hear whispering and giggling.

"I bet Mum wants to join in with Twister," said Rosie in a quiet voice. "She keeps telling me that it's one of her favourite games."

"You should let her. It'll be fun," I said. I couldn't see either of my parents wanting to join in with something like that. But Rosie's mum is pretty cool.

"It's *embarrassing*!" Rosie hissed, just as her mum came back into the

97

kitchen.

"What's embarrassing?" she asked.

"Me always wearing my football shirt," I said quickly.

"It's not embarrassing," laughed Rosie's mum. "If that's what you want to wear, then you go right ahead and wear it Kenny. Stand up for what you believe in, that's what I say." Rosie rolled her eyes.

"Anyway, thank you girls," Rosie's mum continued, taking a pile of plates from Fliss. "You go into the lounge and do whatever you're going to do. I might join in with Twister myself!"

"What did I tell you?" Rosie muttered under her breath.

We grabbed our torches and stumbled across the hall into the lounge. When Rosie opened the door, there was a loud blast of music and a flash of coloured lights. It looked like a proper disco! Mega-cool or what!

CHAPTER NINE

Rosie's dad, Adam and Spud were at the far end of the lounge. They all had great goofy grins on their faces.

"I thought there was a power cut!" shouted Rosie above the Spice Girls, who were blaring out from the cassette player.

"There was, but the electricity came on again just before you had your meal," explained Rosie's dad. "Your mum thought it would be nice if we surprised you with all this."

The Christmas lights, which were strung up around the walls, were flashing in time to the music.

"Spud helped me with those," said Mr Cartwright, "and Adam helped with the music, didn't you son?" Adam grinned and nodded.

"It's brill!" Rosie gave her dad and Adam a big kiss, and punched Spud on the arm in a friendly way.

Rosie's mum and Tiff had appeared in the doorway.

"Thanks Mum!" Rosie called and blew her a kiss.

Her mum smiled and said, "But I thought we were going to play Twister!"

"Later Mum!" Rosie laughed and pulled a face at the rest of us.

Rosie's dad didn't look as though he was the kind of man who likes to dance. He looked a bit embarrassed watching us too. I'm a fling-myself-all-over-the-room kind of dancer, and when I'd trodden on his toes a few times he decided that it was time he made a move. As far away from us as possible!

"Bye girls! Have a good party!" he called. Rosie looked disappointed to see him leaving. I think she thought it was nice to have all her family round her for once. I guess she wants her parents to get back together, but I don't think they will. They seem kind of happy without each other.

"Thanks Mr Cartwright!" we shouted to Rosie's dad. "This is wicked!" Rosie just stood there looking sad.

"Come on Rosie! Get with the groove!" I shouted and got her dancing again.

At least Adam was smiling again. He was kind of whizzing backwards and forwards in his wheelchair as though he was dancing with us.

"Hey, what have you got there?" I asked him. He had a box resting on his knee. He moved closer so that I could see it. It was a CD-Rom all about football. It was way cool!

"You lucky thing! Did your dad bring it for you?" I asked. Adam nodded.

"Monster!"

Adam is really hot on the computer. He has a good one because it's a kind of therapy for him. Rosie and Tiff use it too of course, but it's in Adam's room and he seems to use it the most. He had to show Rosie's mum how to use it when she started college, which we all thought was funny. It's usually parents who show their kids how to do stuff isn't it? But with computers it always seems to be the other way round!

"Did Dad bring you that because he didn't take you fishing?" asked Rosie dancing up to us. Adam nodded.

"That's not fair is it?" she said grumpily.

"He probably realised how disappointed Adam was," I said.

"Yeah well. It's not the same is it?" Rosie said crossly.

"Chill out!" I laughed. "Adam's happy *and* your dad set all this up," I said pointing to the lights. "You can't have a downer on him today!" Rosie looked a bit guilty. "Suppose not," she said and danced over to the others.

"Aren't we playing Twister then?" called out Mrs Cartwright.

"No Mum!" laughed Rosie.

"Well anyway, 'dancing's what I want, what I really really want'," sang Rosie's mum in time to the music. "I think I love dancing more than I love Twister, anyway."

Rosie groaned but you could tell that she was secretly pleased that her mum was so trendy. And her mum was brill. You'd think *she* was the schoolgirl, the way she screamed with laughter all the time. But she wasn't embarrassing or anything. I still think that Rosie sometimes wishes her mum would act her age more.

After she'd been dancing for half an hour or so, Mrs Cartwright flopped onto the settee. "Phew! I'm exhausted. I think I need a lie-down!" she gasped, "and speaking of lying down..." She looked at her watch, "it's almost nine now. Another half an hour then it's time you lot started making tracks upstairs."

"Aw Mum! You said ten!" pleaded Rosie, looking at her mum with her eyes all wide.

"Don't push it my girl!" laughed her mum. "If you're good – we'll see!"

"Cool!" we all yelled and did high fives.

Rosie's mum went out and we expected Tiff and Spud to follow, but they didn't, they stayed behind.

"It's alright," Rosie told them. "We're not going to wreck the place. We don't need to be chaperoned any more!"

"We thought we might stay, actually. This *is* my cassette you're playing," mumbled Tiff.

We were listening to Oasis, which was class. Tiff and Spud started dancing – if you could call it that. Spud sort of jerked around the floor and Tiff shuffled along behind him. Very strange! Rosie shrugged her shoulders as if to say 'I'm sorry about them, but what can I do?' But the rest of us didn't mind. The more the merrier, and Tiff and Spud were alright really. Adam stayed for a short while, but then Rosie's mum came in to get him ready for bed. He sort of waved 'Goodbye' to us all. I'm glad that he'd joined in with our party.

Time seems to flash past when you're having fun doesn't it? We couldn't believe it when Rosie's mum came in and told us that it was nearly ten. Lyndz was starting to look a bit dopey and Fliss had been slumped on the settee for the last fifteen minutes or so. But the rest of us were full of beans and ready to dance the night away.

"Not in this house you don't!" laughed Rosie's mum. "Right, quick sticks, upstairs and ready for bed. And I don't want to hear a peep out of you."

She looked at us and laughed. "Some hope!"

We'd had a great day. Better than we'd expected when we first arrived. And everyone seemed really happy, especially Rosie.

"Great party, Rosie!" said Frankie, when we got up to the bedroom.

"Yeah, monster!" I agreed.

Fliss and Lyndz had already crashed out on the bed, but they mumbled their appreciation too.

Speaking of crashing out on the bed, we hadn't decided who was going to sleep where. When we have a sleepover at Rosie's, three of us manage to fit on her double bed and the other two have to sleep on the floor. It's only fair that Rosie has the bed seeing as it's her house, and the rest of us usually toss for it. Only this time it looked as though Fliss and Lyndz were already settled down for the night. They still had to get undressed and do all the bathroom stuff. But even I wasn't mean enough to make them sleep on the floor.

"It looks like you and me kid!" I said to Frankie in my fake American accent. She just groaned. Cheeky thing!

I can't work Fliss out sometimes. We virtually had to carry her into the bathroom because she was so tired, but when we got back into our sleeping bags and someone mentioned the magic words, "Is it time for our presents now?" Whoosh! She was wide-awake and raring to go.

"Presents! I'd almost forgotten about our presents! Go and get them Rosie!" she yelled.

"OK. Keep your hair on!" said Rosie and felt under her pillow for the room's key.

"Right, who's the joker?" she demanded. "Whoever's got the key, can you give it back now? Please."

We all looked at each other. Or rather everyone looked at me. I do sometimes hide things for a joke, I'll admit. But not this time. Besides, I'd never been alone in the bedroom, so I couldn't have taken the key. Come to think of it, we'd all been together since we got there. Apart from Fliss. She'd been by herself for half an hour or more when we left her during Hide and Seek.

"OK Fliss, we know you've got it. Hand it over!" I said, half-joking. We were all totally gob-smacked when Fliss went very red and started to cry.

CHAPTER TEN

"I haven't got the key," Fliss sobbed. "I *did* look for it when you lot left me during Hide and Seek, but I couldn't find it. I'm sorry."

"Well what would you have done if you had found it?" I demanded.

"I don't know. Just felt the presents I suppose," Fliss mumbled through her sniffs.

"That's a bit sneaky Fliss," said Frankie. "We were all supposed to get our presents together."

"And now none of us can get them because we've lost the key," said Rosie crossly.

"Look I've said I'm sorry, haven't I?" cried Fliss. "I wouldn't have taken them or anything."

"I know you wouldn't," said Rosie more gently. "Maybe the key fell off the bed when you were feeling for it." We all got down on our hands and knees and shone our torches under the bed. The key wasn't there, but there were several large gaps between the floorboards.

"Maybe it's fallen down there," said Frankie.

We pushed Rosie's bed to one side and Rosie shone her torch down the gaps. "I can see it!" she said. "Who's going to put their hand down to pull it out?"

We all looked at Fliss. She'd got us into this mess, and she probably had the smallest hands to get us out!

"It feels all dusty and horrible!" she grumbled as she fished about under the floorboards.

"Yeah, watch out for the mice!" I laughed.

Fliss, who had just grabbed hold of the key, screamed, pulled her arm out of the floorboards and let go of the key. CLINK! We heard it landing somewhere at the other side of the room.

"Oh well done Fliss!" I snarled.

"It was your fault for making me jump!" she snapped back.

"Oh for goodness sake stop it you two!" said Frankie. "I can see the key by the door." She went and picked it up. "There. Right, who's for presents?"

"ME!" we all shouted.

"I'll get them," said Rosie. She took the key from Frankie and crept out of the door.

When she was out of the room, Mrs Cartwright came in.

"Not in bed yet girls?" she asked. "I thought you might need these." She tipped a carrier bag on to the bed. Our midnight feast!

"Thanks Mrs Cartwright!" we said.

"That's OK. Just don't make yourselves sick. And don't stay awake too long. Where's Rosie-Posie?"

"Here!" Rosie had just come back into the bedroom, carrying the plastic sack full of presents.

"Ooh, your presents!" said her mum, smiling. "I might stay to watch you opening those!"

One look at Rosie's face made her change her mind!

"On second thoughts, I could do with going to bed. Have fun! And try not to make too much noise!" Mrs Cartwright went out, closing the door behind her.

"Why don't we have our midnight feast while we open our presents?" asked Frankie. "It'll be cool!"

We all went to sit on Rosie's bed and spread the sweets out in the middle. There were Black Jacks, fizzy fish, rhubarb and crumble sweets, a Mars bar, some Doritos and a big bag of popcorn. Scrummy!

As we started to munch into

everything, Rosie delved into her sack and pulled out the first present.

"Frankie!" she announced, and tossed a parcel towards her. It looked quite big and lumpy. It was impossible to guess what it might be.

"Go on! Open it!" shouted Fliss.

"No, I'm going to wait until we've all got our presents, then we can open them together," said Frankie. Typical! I'd have ripped into mine straight away. Now we'd *all* have to wait until everyone had got one.

"Come on then Rosie. Hurry up!" I was getting as bad as Fliss!

Rosie handed a big, flat parcel to Lyndz. It looked quite heavy, but you couldn't tell what it was. She kept a scrunched up parcel for herself which sort of rattled when she touched it. When she gave Fliss hers, you could tell she was just dying to open it. She kept squeezing it and putting it close to her ear and shaking it. I had to turn away because I was dying to laugh and

I didn't want her to know that it was from me. My present was the last out of the sack. It was soft and squashy, but it kind of rattled too, in a muffled sort of way.

"On your marks! Get set!" shouted Rosie, her parcel in her hand. "GO!"

We all ripped into the brown paper. My present had about a whole roll of sellotape on it, so it wasn't easy to get at.

"Look at this! My own baby sister!" shrieked Frankie. She was holding a gross-looking baby doll. It was all squashy and looked as though it was about to puke any minute. But Frankie loved it.

"Look it's got a bottle too. Can I fill it with water?" she yelled and rushed out to the bathroom.

"Whoever bought her that got it right!" I laughed. "But you do realise, we'll now have a sixth member of the Sleepover Club. She'll take it everywhere with her!"

"I'd never have thought of that for Frankie," said Fliss. "She always seems too grown up for dolls!"

Frankie rushed back into the room,

"Look at this!" she yelled. "It's so cool!"

She gave the baby its bottle and it started to wee.

"Oh gross!" I said. Only Frankie could be thrilled with that.

"Oh wow!" gasped Fliss. "Look at these bangles. Wicked! I saw these in Miss Selfridge. They're brill! You got them for me didn't you, Rosie? Thanks, they're great!"

Monster! She actually thought that someone had bought them! Fortunately when she said that I had just opened my present, which was a wicked pair of Leicester City socks. I shoved them in my mouth to stop myself laughing at Fliss, and I nearly choked on the Fox keyring, which was wrapped up inside them.

"Oh man! This is so cool!" I

shrieked, bouncing up and down on Rosie's bed. I looked round at the others, but it was impossible to tell who had bought them for me.

"I bet this was from you Fliss, wasn't it?" asked Rosie. She was looking at some frosted eyeshadow, and matching lipstick and nail varnish. Fliss blushed and nodded.

"Thank you!" said Rosie hugging her. "I always have to borrow Tiff's make-up and now I've got some of my very own!"

Lyndz was still trying to unfasten her present. Frankie leaned across to help her. When they finally ripped off the paper, we could see that it was a handmade wooden door plaque, which read: 'LYNDZ'S ROOM'. Underneath someone had painted: 'Keep Out Stuart, Tom, Ben and Spike'.

"This is great!" yelled Lyndz. "Now they've no excuse to barge into my room!"

We looked at each other's presents

and tried to guess who had bought them. But apart from Fliss admitting that she'd bought Rosie's make-up, no one was letting on.

Frankie was still shaking with laughter at her doll, when Mrs Cartwright appeared. She was in her dressing gown and had taken her make-up off. She didn't look quite as young and trendy as she usually did. And she sounded very tired.

"Come on you lot! Some of us have assignments to finish tomorrow!" she sighed.

"Sorry!" we all said, and got into our sleeping bags.

"Night!" she called and turned the light out. We counted to twenty-five, then turned on our torches.

"Thanks for a great party Rosie," Frankie whispered.

"It has been good hasn't it?" Rosie whispered back. And it had. After a lousy start!

We sang our Club song, turned off

our torches and settled down to sleep. Frankie had her sleeping bag right next to mine on the floor.

"Did you get me my socks?" I whispered.

"I'm not saying anything," she laughed. I thought she might have done, but then I thought that I recognised her writing on Lyndz's plaque.

"Who do you think bought you the doll?" I asked, but she was already asleep. I could see her 'baby' tucked up beside her. Sweet! A bit sad, but sweet all the same!

The next morning when we woke up – wouldn't you know it, – the sun was shining! We played the outdoor games we should have played at the party. Then, after breakfast, it was time for us to go. Fliss's mum came to collect Fliss and Lyndz. Fliss was wearing her bracelets. I was well-chuffed about that, but I didn't let on that I'd made them. What she doesn't know won't hurt her, as Frankie's gran says.

Frankie and I walked home together. We were already planning what we should do for our twentieth birthday sleepover! We agreed that Rosie's party had been pretty cool, and that the bad things like the rain and the power cut are what had made it special. It just goes to show that however much you plan something, it never turns out as you expect it to.

So now you know all about our tenth birthday sleepover party! Come on, I'll race you to Frankie's! She's going to be so mad when she finds out that I've already told you all about it. But too much talking would only have made her sore throat worse! I reckon she only got it because she shrieked so much over that stupid doll. I wonder if she's figured out who gave it to her yet. I *think* I might have worked out who gave everybody their presents but I'm not completely sure. What do you think?

Come on! Last one to Frankie's is a pile of slime!

Sleepover Girls on Horseback

An imprint of HarperCollinsPublishers

CHAPTER ONE

Hi there. Do you want to come and see the horses with me? That's where I'm going now. Look, I know you're thinking, Lyndz is going to bore us with all that dreary stable stuff! The rest of the Sleepover Club used to think that as well. *And* tut and sigh and make neighing noises. But not any more. Not after our latest adventure. In fact, they're coming to see the horses too. I'm going to meet them there – honest!

I haven't told you before, but I have a riding lesson once a week and I help out at the local stables whenever I can. I don't talk about it *too* much in front of the others because they start getting bored and yawn a lot. Still, when you hear about their riding experiences, it's not surprising really. Take Fliss for a start.

Whenever I even *mention* mucking out, she puts her hands over her ears and starts squealing. She's far too anxious about staying clean and tidy to get involved in things like that! Actually I enjoy all those bits – the mucking out and the grooming – almost as much as the riding. You feel kind of close to the horses and they smell all sort of sweet and leathery and warm.

Sorry, there I go again! Where was I? Oh yes, Fliss. She can be a bit of a wimp sometimes and she actually admits that she's frightened of horses. I suppose I *can* sort of understand that – they are kind of big. But they're just so gentle! Even Fliss understands that now, but boy did she find out the hard way! I think we all feel a bit guilty about what happened, but she's OK now.

Frankie is more sensible. She went for riding lessons with Kenny once. Can you imagine that? Kenny on a horse acting the fool and pretending to be a cowboy! It was all "Yee-ha!" and "Hi Ho, Silver!"

You know Kenny: she always wants to do everything as fast as she can. She expected to be out hacking on her first lesson and jumping fences by her second. She just didn't realise that riding isn't like that. It's all about communicating with the horse. You and the horse have to work as a team. Riding is *very* hard work. And Kenny doesn't like hard work at the best of times. So she gave up.

Frankie lasted a bit longer, but you could tell that she wasn't in love with horses in the way I am. I think you really *do* have to love them to want to work at getting everything right. You have so much to think about – squeezing your legs here, holding the reins there, sitting just so. It's not just about trotting along and looking pretty. Which is just as well because I *never* look pretty.

9

That's what my four stupid brothers tell me anyway. Even Spike, and he's only a baby!

Rosie is the fifth member of the Sleepover Club and she didn't take to riding either. She went along after her brother, Adam, started. You rememer Adam, don't you? He's a year older than Rosie and has cerebral palsy. Riding is a form of therapy for him. He started going once a week with his school and when his mum realised how much it was helping him, she arranged for him to go with two of his friends on another afternoon.

He rides at the same stables as me. Mrs McAllister, who owns it, is a qualified instructor for the Riding for the Disabled Association. She's brilliant because as well as knowing everything there is to know about horses, she knows exactly what kind of horse someone like Adam needs to ride. She says that a little pony like Bramble would have too choppy a stride, so he goes on Marvel, who is a chestnut mare. Her walk is much smoother, but Adam still has to squeeze his legs very hard to make her obey his commands. And when you think about it that's really tough for Adam because he spends all day in a wheelchair so he's not using his leg muscles at all. Just balancing on Marvel gives him a really tough workout.

Crikey, I sound like some kind of doctor, don't I? Kenny would be proud of me!

Adam was so thrilled about riding Marvel, he told Rosie all about it. Of course, *she* wanted to have a go then. She was put on Alfie, the most gorgeous bay with a white star on his forehead and eyelashes to die for, but poor Rosie just couldn't get it together at all. First she had trouble mounting him, then her legs wouldn't stay in the right position in the stirrups. And Alfie just did his own thing, no matter what Rosie tried to tell him to do. In the end she told her mum that riding wasn't for her and she never went again.

I bet you're wondering what this has to do with our latest adventure, aren't you? Well, quite a lot actually – come with me to the stables and I'll tell you all about it on the way.

It started when we were round at Rosie's one afternoon after school. We were working on some dumb geography project.

"I don't know why Mrs Weaver doesn't just send us all on holiday if she wants us to find out about other countries," snarled Kenny, stuffing yet another chocolate biscuit into her mouth.

"Yes, I wouldn't mind a week on the beach in Barbados," sighed Frankie.

"Or a trip to Disneyland!" yelled Fliss.

"That's not a country, stupid!" laughed Kenny.

"I know that, smartypants!" snapped Fliss. "I've been to EuroDisney. I'd just like to go to Disneyland in America to see if it's any different, that's all!"

"Ooh! Hark at her!" we all screeched together, pulling faces at each other.

Fliss hates it when we make fun of her, even though she usually deserves it. She flung her pencil case at Kenny and all her felt pens sort of burst out, scattering around the kitchen. We all creased up and scrambled on to the floor to pick them up. We were scrabbling about under the table, when we heard the front door close.

"That'll be Mum and Adam," said Rosie.

We waited for Adam to burst into the kitchen in his wheelchair like he usually did. But he didn't. All we could hear were lots of strange wailing sounds coming from the hall.

"Oh no!" gasped Rosie. "That's Adam. It sounds like he's really upset about something."

We rushed into the hall to see what was wrong. Rosie's mum was crouched over Adam, trying to calm him down, but we could tell just by looking at him that something awful had happened.

"What is it, Mum? What's wrong?" asked Rosie anxiously. "Is Adam OK?"

Her mum nodded, but carried on stroking Adam's arm. "He's just heard some bad news," she said softly.

"What sort of bad news?" shrieked Rosie. She'd gone completely white and her eyes looked as though they were going to burst out of her head. The rest of us sort of hung back in case it was a private thing.

"We've just heard that there's been a very bad fire at the riding school," said Rosie's mum.

"Oh no!" I gasped. For a minute I felt as though I couldn't breathe. I sat down on the stairs. "What happened? Are the horses safe?" I asked. My voice sounded kind of wobbly. It didn't sound like my voice at all.

"Yes, Lyndz, the horses were in the fields when it happened. And they're all perfectly safe."

"What about Mrs McAllister, is she all right?" asked Frankie.

"Yes, everyone is fine, thank goodness," sighed Mrs Cartwright. "It could have been much worse. Just imagine what would have happened if the horses had been in the stables when the fire started."

I didn't want to imagine that. All I could

think of was Marvel and Alfie and Bramble and all the other beautiful horses. What was going to happen to them now? It felt like the worst day of my life.

When Rosie's mum had taken Adam upstairs for his bath, we went back into the kitchen. It was as though a huge grey blanket of sadness had been dropped on top of us. Nobody spoke for ages.

"There must be *something* we can do to help," I said suddenly. I couldn't bear the silence any longer and just thinking that we could be useful in some way made me feel a bit better. "Let's go to the stables and see what we can do."

"Shouldn't we call Mrs McAllister first?" asked Fliss. "Maybe she won't want anyone there."

"Fliss is right," agreed Frankie. "Why don't you ring Mrs McAllister when you get home, Lyndz, and if she wants us to help, we'll all come to the stables with you later in the week, won't we?"

Everyone nodded. Everyone except Fliss.

15

"You'll come and help too, won't you, Fliss?" Frankie dug her hard in the ribs.

"Ouch! I suppose so. But I don't want to go anywhere near the horses," said Fliss, rubbing her side.

"OK, that's agreed. You check things with Mrs McAllister, Lyndz. Then it's the Sleepover Club to the rescue!" laughed Kenny and pretended to play a fanfare.

We all laughed too. It sounded like one of our silly jokes. Only this time it was real.

CHAPTER TWO

"Well, what did she say?" The others crowded round me when I got to school the next day.

"Who?" I pretended to look blank, but I couldn't fool them.

"Mrs McAllister of course! Come on, Lyndz. Spill!" commanded Frankie.

"Mum rang her for me," I admitted. "She thought that Mrs McAllister might be in a state of shock."

Kenny's eyes lit up at the thought of some medical-type complaint to deal with.

"And was she?" she asked eagerly.

"Nope, it sounded like she was very calm actually," I said.

Kenny looked disappointed.

"When did the fire start?" asked Frankie, getting down to serious matters.

"Quite early in the morning. The horses were in the fields and Mrs McAllister had gone to check on them," I explained. "She said that something caught her eye. She looked up and saw smoke coming from the stable block. She ran back to see what was happening, but when she got there, three of the stables had burnt completely and the roofs on the others were still burning. She called the fire brigade, grabbed the fire extinguishers, and put out what she could."

"But what caused the fire to start in the first place?" asked Fliss.

"Mrs McAllister doesn't know for sure. She thinks a delivery man must have dropped a cigarette," I told them. "There are huge 'No Smoking' signs all around the stables – how could anyone be so careless?" I looked round and realised that for once I had everyone's attention. And knowing the Sleepover Club you realise what a miracle that is. We usually all chatter at once.

"Do you think someone did it on purpose?" asked Kenny suddenly. "Someone might want to get rid of the riding school! Maybe the owner of a rival stables is trying to close down all the competition so everyone will have to go to them for riding lessons."

Uh-oh! Kenny was on one of her fantasy trips again.

"Get real!" laughed Frankie. "I don't know if you've noticed, but we live in Cuddington, not Hollywood. Things like that don't happen around here."

The others started to laugh and tease Kenny.

"Hey, Lyndz, are you all right?" asked Rosie. "You've gone very quiet."

I'd tried to be bright and happy and everything. But I kept thinking of something else that mum had said last night. She'd asked Mrs McAllister where the horses were being kept.

"On Mr Brocklehurst's farm – for the moment," she'd told her.

That was great news for me, because my brother, Stuart, helps out there. And the horses have always grazed in some of Mr Brocklehurst's fields anyway.

"Aw, we could have had some of the horses to stay here in our garden!" I'd said. Wouldn't that have been great? We've got a huge garden and I'd have looked after them ever so well.

"They might have to live in someone's garden if what Mrs McAllister says is true," Mum had told me. "She says that rebuilding the stables is going to cost thousands of pounds – she just doesn't have that kind of money and only some of it is covered by insurance. She needs the horses settled before winter, so it looks like she might have to close down the riding school and sell the horses."

I had been so upset that I'd hardly slept. And I nearly started crying when I told the others.

"But what about Adam?" Rosie blurted out. "He was upset enough about the fire. I don't know how he'll cope if he can't ride any more."

"Mrs McAllister's going to carry on with her lessons for the moment," I told her. "The practice ring wasn't damaged and it's right next to the farm so the horses can get there easily."

"Are there any other stables nearby?" Fliss asked.

"None that do Riding for the Disabled," Rosie said. "Mum's already asked."

"I don't want to go to another stables. I want to go to that one!" I shouted. The others looked shocked. They're not used to seeing me get upset. But then, nothing has ever threatened the horses before.

"OK, OK, calm down." Frankie took control, as usual. "I'm sure there's *something* we can do."

But before we could come up with a plan, the bell went for the start of school.

"Right you lot, this is Operation Horseback!" shouted Frankie in her Sergeant-Major voice. "*Rendez-vous* here at 10.30 hours (that means first break, dummies). And get your brains into gear for a plan of action. Right you 'orrible lot. Quick march – left, right, left, right…" and we all marched into the classroom.

We would have marched right to our chairs, but Mrs Weaver gave us one of her looks. Sometimes she has no sense of humour. I think she must have had one of her headaches.

I tried to concentrate on my work but I couldn't. I just had to think of a way to save Mrs McAllister's riding school. Every time I looked across at Rosie she seemed to be deep in thought, too. Fliss was staring into space a lot, but I think that was just because she couldn't understand the maths we were doing.

At first break we all met up in the playground.

"Any ideas?" asked Frankie.

We all shook our heads.

"If we were on one of those dumb TV programmes, we'd rebuild the stables ourselves!" she sighed. "But I can't see us being much good at that."

"It's a pity they don't have a Stable Building badge in Brownies. We could have done it for that!" laughed Kenny. She jumped on Frankie's back and pretended to ride her round the playground.

"No horseplay, girls! Someone will get hurt!" shouted out Mrs Daniels.

Frankie had a fit of the giggles. "Horseplay!" she screamed. "Horseplay!"

She was laughing so much that Kenny couldn't hold on and fell to the ground. But she was laughing too, so it didn't matter.

"I bet Danny-Boy didn't even say it on purpose," Kenny snorted. "She's had a sense of humour bypass that woman!"

"We don't have to actually *build* the stables, do we?" said Fliss, suddenly concerned.

"What?" asked the rest of us together.

23

"Talk about a sense of humour bypass, Fliss – were you operated on too?" asked Kenny.

"No, stupid!" said Fliss going pink. "What I meant was, it's not *building* the stables that's the problem, is it? You said that Mrs McAllister doesn't have any money. So really we should try to find her someone who has."

"Right, Fliss. I'll just write to the Queen shall I?" said Kenny. "*Dear Queenie, the stables where our friends ride have been burnt down. Please send us lots of money so that we can build some more. Lots of love, the Sleepover Club.* That should do the trick, shouldn't it? Ten pound notes will be falling through the letter box in no time!"

"Ha, ha, ha!" said Fliss, going pinker than ever. "That's not what I meant, but there must be *someone* who can help."

"Fliss is right," said Frankie. "Why don't we think of ways to raise money?"

"But we'd never raise enough!" said Fliss.

"That's not the point," said Frankie firmly.

"Every little helps. I'm sure there are lots of people who don't know that the stables have burnt down. If we can 'raise people's awareness', as Mum says, maybe they'll make a donation and Mrs McAllister will get enough money to rebuild her stables."

Suddenly I felt cheerful again. It really seemed as though we *could* make a difference. And more importantly, it looked as though Alfie, Bramble and Marvel wouldn't have to be sold to someone else.

"I'm going to the farm after school tomorrow," I told the others. "I'll tell Mrs McAllister that we're going to help. I'm sure she'll be pleased."

"We'll all come with you, Lyndz," said Frankie. "If the Sleepover Club are going to the rescue, we really should find out what we're rescuing!"

"Yeah!" shouted Kenny and Rosie, doing high fives.

"Are you coming too?" I asked Fliss. She was being very quiet and I knew she wasn't wild about horses. "You don't have to if you don't want to."

"Of course I am!" she said crossly. "You're not leaving me out!"

So we arranged to meet at Mr Brocklehurst's farm after school the next day. It seemed like such a good idea at the time. We should have realised then that Fliss and horses really don't mix!

CHAPTER THREE

I was really excited about going to Mr Brocklehurst's farm the next day, but I was kind of nervous too. I hadn't seen the horses since the fire you see. What if they'd changed? What if they were really spooked by what had happened and wouldn't let anyone near them?

"Are you sure the horses are all right?" I asked Stuart, as Dad drove us to the farm.

"For the hundredth time, Lyndz, they're fine," Stuart replied.

That made me feel a bit better, but butterflies were still flapping about inside my tummy. I know it sounds crazy, but it's just because I love those horses more than anything else in the world and I was worried that they'd be feeling frightened because their routine had changed. Horses are creatures of habit you see.

When we arrived at the farm, I said bye to Dad and jumped out to open the gate. The first thing I saw was Alfie in the field. He was munching grass as usual and didn't look worried at all.

"Happy now?" asked Stuart.

"Yep!" I nodded.

"Oh look, isn't that one of your mad friends?" Stuart pointed to the lane leading to the practice ring. Rosie was standing there, waving at me like a crazy woman. I started walking towards her. Suddenly, *thud*! Kenny leapt on to my back.

"Hiya, Lyndz! Have I missed anything? I would've got here earlier, but my stupid sister wanted to come too. I had to bribe her to stay away. She took all my chocolate and made me promise to help with the washing up for a week!" Kenny was all out of breath and red in the face. And so was I, with such a great lump on top of me!

"Gerroff!" I yelled and threw her off.

"Girls! That's not very lady-like behaviour!" said a loud voice behind us. It sounded just like Mrs Poole, our headmistress. I turned round in a panic, but it was only Frankie. She's dead good at voices.

"What are you doing? I thought we were supposed to be asking Mrs McAllister how we could help," said Frankie. She can be too serious sometimes. She'd probably chill out a bit more if she had brothers and sisters to deal with. I'm always telling her that she can have *my* brothers any time!

"I don't think she'd like us disturbing her now. She's taking a ride with Adam and his friends," said Rosie.

We had walked back down the path and were standing by the field, looking at Alfie.

"All that stuff in the ring is so boring!" said Kenny. "You see Alfie? I bet I could make him jump over that fence – no problem!"

"Oh yeah!" Frankie and Rosie said, laughing.

I don't trust Kenny sometimes. She has a wild streak in her and you just don't know what she's going to do next. I could tell that she was in Grand National mode and I had to get her away from Alfie – fast! Fortunately, just then Stuart walked past, wearing his big wellies and smelling of pigs.

"You're not frightening the horses are you?" he shouted.

"Ha, ha, ha!" we said together.

"Actually," he said, coming over to us, "what exactly *are* you doing here? You're not planning anything are you, Lyndz? I have to work here, remember. I don't want you causing any trouble."

"As if!" I said. He snorted and walked off.

We climbed on to the fence and sat looking at Alfie as he munched away at the grass.

"Did you know that horses graze between sixteen and twenty hours a day?" I asked.

"That sounds nice. I could manage that myself!" laughed Kenny.

"It's because they've got small stomachs you see. They can't cope with big meals," I explained.

"Sounds like Fliss, she's always nibbling at her food!" laughed Rosie. "She hasn't got such big teeth though. And I've never seen her eat grass."

"I bet her mum has!" said Frankie. "She's always going on those weird diets, and there can't be many calories in grass!"

"Speaking of Fliss, where is she?" I asked. "Do you think she's chickened out of coming after all?"

"Horsied out you mean!" shrieked Kenny.

I don't know why, but that really made me laugh. And you know what happens when I laugh too much, don't you? Yep, I got the dreaded hiccups.

"Aw, Lyndz, look, you're frightening Alfie!" laughed Rosie.

Alfie was looking at me through his long eyelashes. He didn't look very impressed.

31

But that only made me laugh more. Frankie grabbed hold of my hand to give me her evil 'thumb in the hand' routine. I was trying to balance on the fence, holding on with only one arm. It wasn't very easy. What I didn't need was someone running up behind me and digging me in the ribs. Which is exactly what Fliss did.

"Lyndz, I'm here!" she shouted.

Thump! I fell off the fence. *Splat*! Right on top of Fliss.

She lay on the ground covered in bits of hay. And pig muck, by the smell of her.

"Lyndz, you clumsy thing! Look at me!" she wailed. "I wasn't going to come in the first place. I wish I hadn't bothered now!"

"I'm sorry, Fliss. I couldn't help it!" I said, pulling her to her feet. "But at least it got rid of my hiccups!"

"Well, that's all right then!" grumbled Fliss.

The rest of us looked at Fliss and started to laugh. She was covered in muddy marks and nasty brown splodges. It wouldn't have been so bad if she'd been wearing scruffy old jeans and wellies like the rest of us. But that's not Fliss's style. Instead, she had on her black Adidas top, new pink bootleg trousers and some high-heeled boots.

"Fliss what *are* you like!" laughed Kenny. "This isn't a photo shoot for *Vogue* you know. You're supposed to be mucking in!"

"Fliss has been mucking in!" shrieked Rosie. "*Pig* mucking in!"

We screamed with laughter again. But we soon stopped when it looked as though Fliss was going to cry.

"I didn't have any old jeans, Mum's given them all away," she spluttered. "And I need some new wellies as well. My feet are too big for the ones I've got."

"You should have said," said Rosie. "I've got some old ones that will probably fit you. *And* some old jeans. They're in a pile waiting for Mum to take to the charity shop."

"I wish I'd known," said Fliss, trying to brush the marks from her trousers. "Anyway, have you come up with a plan to raise millions of pounds yet?"

"Nope!" said Kenny, Rosie and I.

"Yes!" shouted Frankie. "Yes, yes, yes!"

We all stared at her with our mouths open.

"I am Brain of Britain. I should have a medal!" she laughed, dancing about. "Don't you see? It's brilliant. We've all got things that we don't need any more, but which someone else probably does. Instead of taking them to the charity shop, *we* can sell them. And the money we make can go towards the Save the Stables campaign. Genius, or what?"

"But how will people find out that we have things to sell?" asked Fliss.

"We'll make posters and put them up all over Cuddington," replied Frankie.

"We need to do it as soon as possible," I said. "The sooner we raise money the better."

Frankie started jumping up and down. She was going quite pink with excitement. "We're having a sleepover at my place next

Friday, aren't we? How about having a sale the next day? In our garden."

"Yes!" we all said together.

"Won't your mum mind?" asked Fliss, nervously.

"Nah! It's for a good cause, and Mum believes in good causes," Frankie replied. "She might even donate some stuff herself."

"Look!" I said. "Mrs McAllister is just coming back from the lesson with Adam. Let's tell her what we're going to do."

Mrs McAllister was leading Adam on Marvel. He looked very tired, but happy. We told her about our plan, all talking at the same time and shouting to make ourselves heard. She just sort of smiled sadly, but Adam became quite excited.

"What's he saying?" we asked Rosie's mum, who had just turned up.

She interpreted the gestures Adam made with his head and arms. "He says that he'll do the posters on his computer for you!" she announced.

"Coo-el!" we all cried. Adam's brilliant at

stuff like that.

"Well, I'm not sure how much good it will do," said Mrs McAllister sadly, "but it's great that you're taking such an interest. I hope it goes well."

"Is there anything you'd like us to do now?" I asked.

"Well, these horses need feeding. Then of course there's the mucking out!" she said.

"Sorry, my dad's here," said Frankie, hurrying away. "You're coming with me, aren't you, Kenny?" Kenny laughed and ran off as well, waving at me as she went.

"We've got to get back too, haven't we, Mum?" said Rosie, pushing Adam towards the car.

"That leaves you and me, Fliss!" I laughed.

"Sorry, Lyndz, Mum's coming for me in five minutes. I think I'll just go and wait by the gate," squealed Fliss, moving away.

Unfortunately, while we had been talking, I hadn't noticed that Marvel had taken a fancy to Fliss's Adidas top. As she walked away there was a loud rip, and a great chunk of black material came away in Marvel's mouth.

You should have seen the look on her face! That should really have been a sign that Fliss should be kept away from horses for good. But unfortunately for Fliss, we didn't take any notice.

CHAPTER FOUR

I was quite tired when I arrived home from the farm. Mucking out horses is hard work you know. For once I didn't have any homework to do, only reading, and I always do that in bed. I just planned to have something to eat and then flop in front of the TV. Bliss!

"There you are, boss!" said Mum as soon as I walked through the door. "I was wondering when you were going to get back. I hope you're going to pay me for being your secretary!"

She's really lost it this time, I thought to

myself. I mean, I know that Mum has a hard time working and looking after five children, but what *was* she on about?

"Your friends have been phoning for the last hour! I thought you were going to see them at the farm," she said.

"I did," I replied, puzzled.

"I wrote down their messages and put them on your desk—"

I started to run up to my bedroom.

"Not so fast, young lady," she called. "Wash your hands and come for supper first. The rest of us are starving!"

I gobbled down my supper so quickly it was a record, even for me. When I rushed into my bedroom, my desk was covered in post-it notes. Mum had stuck them in a line so I knew which order to read them in. The first message read:

From Frankie:
What happened to Fliss's top? I was going to come back to find out, but Kenny wouldn't let me in case we got roped into mucking out!

The next note said:

Can Lyndz come over to my place after school tomorrow? Adam wants to find out what we want him to put on the posters – Rosie

Mum had written underneath:

WHICH POSTERS? WHAT ARE YOU UP TO, LYNDSEY COLLINS?

The next message was from Kenny:

Are you going to Rosie's tomorrow? I am, and Frankie is too. Have you spoken to Fliss since her 'horsey' experience? Ha, ha, ha! (That was Kenny laughing.)
I HOPE YOU'RE NOT UPSETTING FLISS AGAIN. I TOLD KENNY THAT YOU COULD GO TO ROSIE'S AFTER SCHOOL. SHE TOLD ME ABOUT THE POSTERS AND THE SALE TO RAISE MONEY FOR THE STABLES. PERHAPS YOU CAN GET RID OF SOME OF THAT JUNK IN YOUR BEDROOM – MUM

The last message was from Fliss:

Mum nearly killed me when she saw the state of my top. She said she always knew that horses were dangerous and she doesn't want me getting mixed up with them. I don't think she's even going to let me go to Rosie's tomorrow – or Frankie's sleepover next week.

I felt really bad when I read that. It was sort of my fault that Fliss had ended up getting so dirty. And if I'd been watching properly, Marvel would never have eaten her top.

There was a knock at my bedroom door. Mum came in.

"Mum, I don't know what to do—" I began.

She handed me another post-it note. It read:

I'VE SPOKEN TO FLISS'S MUM. FLISS CAN GO TO ROSIE'S AND FRANKIE'S. JUST KEEP HER AWAY FROM HORSES FOR GOODNESS' SAKE! – MUM xxx

I read her note and smiled. I grabbed a pen and wrote on the bottom:

Thanks, Mum. You're the best!

When we saw each other at school the next day, we didn't really talk about what had happened at the farm. All our parents had told us to be nice to Fliss, so we didn't want to upset her again. I think she was a bit embarrassed about it too, because she never mentioned it either. And you know Fliss, she usually goes on and on about stuff.

After school we all walked back to Rosie's house. Tiff, her older sister, looks after her until her mum gets back. Her mum's at college at the moment, you see. She's training to be a nursery assistant. She also has to go and pick up Adam from school, so she always gets home a bit later than Rosie.

When we got to her house, Rosie gave us all some Coca-Cola. We put some crisps into a bowl and took them up to her bedroom. Her room's enormous, but it's still not decorated. That's cool because it means we can write on the walls, but she's nearly run out of wall to write on now.

"What are you going to take to the sale?" Frankie asked Rosie.

"I don't know, clothes I suppose," she replied. "I don't really have anything else that I want to get rid of. What about you?"

"Toys that I don't need any more," Frankie said. "I've kept them in case I got a baby brother or sister to give them to, but I don't suppose I ever will now."

The rest of us looked at each other and pulled faces. Frankie could go on for hours about how unfair it is being an only child.

"What are you going to sell, Lyndz?" Kenny asked me, trying to change the subject.

"Dunno," I shrugged. "Mum reckons that I should sell some of the junk I've got in my bedroom. She just doesn't realise that I need it all."

"Same with me," admitted Kenny. "My mum doesn't see why I have to keep all my old football magazines and programmes and stuff. I keep telling her that one day I'll be able to sell them and make a fortune."

"Yeah, right!" I laughed. "Like who would want them?"

A word of warning to you – NEVER criticise Kenny's obsession with Leicester City Football Club. It's just not worth it!

"All right then," she said, looking very angry. "Why are you holding on to all your old posters and horse magazines? If you cared so much about Mrs McAllister's horses, you'd sell them to raise money for the stables."

Aargh! What she was saying was true, but I didn't want to get rid of them.

"All right, I'll sell them," I told her bravely. "As long as you sell your football stuff."

Kenny went bright red. She realised that she'd talked herself into trouble. But Kenny never likes to admit that she's wrong.

"All right, I will!" she said.

Frankie, Rosie and Fliss looked at each other, but they didn't dare say anything. Kenny and I looked at each other. I felt bad and I knew that Kenny did too, but we couldn't go back on our word now.

Just then, we heard the front door open and the sound of Adam's wheelchair speeding across the hall floor.

"We'd better go down," said Rosie. "Adam will be dying to get on with the posters."

We trooped downstairs, still hardly daring to speak to each other.

"Hi, Adam. Have you had a good day?" asked Frankie.

Adam nodded and smiled his big smile. He wheeled himself over to his computer and we all crowded round.

"Right. What shall we put on these posters?" he gestured.

"We'll have to say what the sale's in aid of," I said.

"As briefly as possible," added Frankie. "We need a catchy slogan or something. Why don't you put 'Save our horses' at the top?"

Adam tapped away on his computer.

"Next write that the sale's at my house, on Saturday," said Frankie. "And the time. What do you think about starting at ten and going on till twelve? Will that give us enough time to get everything ready?"

We all nodded.

"You should call it a car boot sale," said Fliss. "People always go to those."

"But it's not is it? There won't *be* any cars there," laughed Kenny. "It's more like a wellington boot sale!"

"Just put 'Grand sale of almost new items'," said Frankie, "and then 'Please support this worthwhile cause' along the bottom."

"We could print them on coloured paper," Rosie suggested. "We want as many people to see them as possible." She put some fluorescent pink paper into the printer, and hey presto! our first poster emerged. It looked awesome:

SAVE OUR HORSES

Help prevent the closure of
McAllister's Riding School

GRAND SALE OF ALMOST NEW ITEMS

at

7 The Ridgeway
Melford Road
Cuddington

Saturday 12th September
10 am - 12 noon

Please support this worthwhile cause

"Adam, you're a genius. Much like myself!" laughed Frankie.

"It's brilliant!" I agreed.

"Coo-el!" the others cheered.

"Now we need to put up as many as possible," said Kenny. "We want to make sure that everyone sees one."

47

Adam printed off a whole load of posters and we took ten each. We figured that as we all live in different parts of the villa₃e, between us we should have the area pretty much covered.

Big mistake!

Why do none of our plans ever turn out the way we want them to?

CHAPTER FIVE

You'd think that it would be easy to get rid of ten posters wouldn't you? Well it wasn't. A lot of the shops in the village actually charge for putting them up in their windows, which is crazy if you ask me.

Frankie decided that she didn't want to put up any posters in school either.

"Why not?" we all asked.

"Because of the M&Ms," she replied. "You know what they're like. They'll spoil it for us."

She was right. The M&Ms – better known as Emma Hughes and Emily Berryman – are our deadly rivals. In front of grown-ups they act so goody-goody it's sickening, but in fact they try to spoil everything we do. We usually get the better of them, but I suppose Frankie was right – we couldn't take the risk this time.

In the end, I put up two posters just outside the school gates. I gave a poster to Ben to put up in his nursery class (but I think he scribbled all over it first), I gave two to Mrs McAllister to put up somewhere at the stables, and stuck the rest on lampposts in our road.

But putting up posters about the sale was the least of my worries. I still had to decide what I was going to sell. I had promised to donate some of my horse posters, but I couldn't decide which ones. I know it sounds silly, but it's as though the horses in the posters are real somehow, so it was really hard for me to decide which ones to give away.

I kept getting out the posters from under my bed and sorting them into two piles –

ones that I loved, and ones that I really really loved. The only problem was that I always ended up with two posters in the first pile, and about thirty-six in the second. Then I felt guilty about leaving those two out to start with, so I put them back with the others anyway. I'm not very good at making decisions.

In the end, Mum helped me make up my mind. She said that the sensible thing to do would be to keep only the most recent posters. The important thing was not to look at them too closely, just decide how long I'd had them.

In the end I had a big pile to take to the sale and a smaller pile to keep. Once I'd decided which posters were going, I put them in a plastic bag and didn't look at them again. Then I did the same thing with all my horse magazines. I felt sad about getting rid of them, but fortunately I had something to take my mind off it. On the Tuesday before her sleepover, Frankie had come rushing into the playground.

"I've had a brilliant idea!" she announced.

"Not another one!" we groaned.

"No, you'll love this!" she said, looking very pleased with herself.

"We're in for a Frankie Thomas special are we?" laughed Kenny. "Go on then. Spill!"

"Well, you know we're having the sale to raise money for the riding school?" she began.

"Are we?" "What sale?" "I didn't know about that!" the rest of us said, pretending to look shocked.

"Ha, ha, ha!" said Frankie. "Well I thought it would be pretty cool if the sleepover had a horsey theme. We could all wear something connected with horses. We can eat cowboy-type food, even our games could be horsey ones. AND whatever you bring for the midnight feast has to fit into the theme too. What do you think?"

"Brilliant!" I laughed, jumping up and down. This sounded like my kind of party.

"Wicked!" said Rosie and Kenny together.

"I don't understand," said Fliss. "You

mean we've got to dress up as a horse?"

"Derr!" said the rest of us, tapping our heads.

"No, Fliss, you can dress as a cowboy or an Indian if you want. Or wear jodhpurs," explained Frankie. "Just use your imagination."

"But I don't think I've got anything like that to wear," moaned Fliss.

"Oh, come on, Fliss," snapped Kenny. "You've got more clothes than the rest of us put together. I'm sure you can find *something*."

We left it so that we wouldn't tell anyone else what we were wearing. It had to be a surprise on Friday night.

I couldn't wait for the sleepover. I love all our sleepovers of course, because we always end up having a wicked time. But it's even more fun if we have to dress up – and I'm really lucky because I've got some ace dressing-up clothes.

I could have worn the jodhpurs that I wear for riding, but they're a bit dirty and smelly. Besides, Mum once made me some of those leather chaps that cowboys wear over their jeans. I love wearing those, and I knew that Kenny would just about die when she saw them.

So on Friday, when I got ready for the sleepover, I put on the chaps and my checked shirt, and Dad lent me one of his bootlace ties. Then I found a beaten-up old leather hat in the dressing-up box. It sort of looked like a cowboy hat. I thought it was pretty cool anyway. The last thing to do was borrow one of Ben's toy guns. I hid it from Mum though, because she doesn't like him having them.

When Dad dropped me off at Frankie's I was so excited I couldn't get out of the car fast enough. I grabbed my sleepover kit and my bag of horse posters and magazines and rushed up to the door. Kenny was already there, looking like the meanest cowboy in the West.

When she heard me, she spun round and said in a fake American accent, "Not so fast pardn'r. This doorway ain't big enough for the both of us!"

We both dropped our bags and grabbed the guns from our holsters. Then we pretended to have this mega shoot-out down Frankie's path. Suddenly the front door opened.

"All right, Butch and Sundance. You'd better come in before the neighbours call the police!" It was Frankie's dad.

Well, Kenny and I just creased up. And it didn't help when Fliss came tiptoeing down the path looking like Little Bo Peep!

"Hic! What are you like, Fliss?" I giggled.

"I'm a cowgirl!" she said angrily. I could tell that she was in a major strop.

"Oh yes, hic! I see now!" I said. She was wearing a flouncy skirt, a white blouse and ankle boots. She didn't look like a cowgirl at all.

"Frankie!" shouted Mr Thomas. "I think Lyndz needs your assistance. She's got hiccups again!"

Frankie came flying downstairs. She

looked pretty cool in a pair of jodhpurs and a riding jacket. Rosie was behind her. She was dressed like an Indian squaw. She said her mum had made her dress out of chamois-leather cloths! It was wicked!

We all looked at each other, shouting "Coo-el!" We didn't mention the fact that Fliss looked as though she'd escaped from the pages of a nursery-rhyme book.

Frankie tried to get rid of my hiccups, but they just wouldn't go away. Eventually her mum appeared.

"I'll give you five pounds if you hiccup again, Lyndz," she said.

The others all stared at me, willing me to make another sound. But do you know, I couldn't!

"Thought that might happen," laughed Frankie's mum, and disappeared again.

We took our things up to Frankie's room, then Kenny asked, "What's the plan then, Buffalo Bill?"

"We're going to do a spot of show jumping, old girl," said Frankie in a put-on snooty voice.

"Jolly good!" we all laughed and traipsed downstairs again, following Frankie out into the garden.

She'd made a sort of obstacle course with planks of wood and things. Frankie pretended to be a horse and Kenny was her rider, then they had to try to get round the course, jumping the fences without falling over. It was hysterical to watch – and even more hysterical to do. We all had a go at being the horse and the rider. Even Fliss, which was a surprise. It was even more surprising when she was quite good at it!

When we'd finished, we flopped on the grass for a bit to get our breath back. Then we played our game where we get into two teams, with one horse and one rider on each team, and each team has to try to knock the other one over. We play that a lot, but this time Frankie said it was like jousting so it was an OK horsey-type game. I was ready for something to eat after that – it's pretty exhausting.

It was getting dark and Frankie's dad had built a small fire in the corner of the garden. We sat round it and helped to cook baked beans and vegebangers. It was wicked!

"We're just like cowboys!" laughed Kenny.

"I expect the plains of America are a bit more rugged than our back garden," said Frankie's dad. "Hang on a minute though." He rushed behind the dustbins and started to howl like a wolf.

"Yes, that's definitely more like it!" said Mrs Thomas, shaking her head and pulling faces at us. "It keeps him happy!" she whispered.

After the baked beans, we toasted marshmallows on long skewers until they were dripping and tasted a bit smoky. Scrummy!

We were all starting to feel a bit drowsy, but Frankie had one more thing for us to do. And this was no game. This was Organising Tomorrow's Big Sale.

CHAPTER SIX

We headed up to Frankie's room and sat on her bed. Frankie took a sheet of paper from her desk. "Look, this is what I thought we'd do tomorrow," she said.

We all crowded round to have a look. It was a sort of timetable:

Get up/breakfast	8 am
Set out tables in garden	9 am
First customers	10 am
Sold up, made lots of money, exhausted and happy!	Midday
Count money	12.10 pm
Clear away	12.20 pm
Chill out, pig out until we're stuffed!	12.40 pm

"Wicked!" we all laughed. "Especially the pigging out bit!"

"So what's everyone going to sell?" asked Frankie.

I raced over to the bunk beds, grabbed the bag containing my posters and magazines and took it back to Frankie's bed. The others were clutching their bags too.

"OK, after three, everyone tip their stuff out!" commanded Kenny. "One... two... three!"

Posters, make-up, toys and clothes spilled out over the bed.

"I hope everything's clean!" said Fliss, picking things up and shaking them as though they were full of dust.

"We don't seem to have much!" said Frankie. She looked very disappointed.

"There are only five of us, Frankie!" said Rosie. "There's only so much stuff we could get rid of."

"Speaking of which," I said, "there don't seem to be many football things here, Kenny."

She gave me an evil stare.

"That's because they're all here," said Frankie. She fished under her bed and found another plastic bag. She tipped lots of posters and programmes on to the bed. There were even a couple of old books about football too.

"Were you trying to hide those, Kenny?" asked Rosie.

"No, I er… well, all right, yes. I just wanted to make sure that Lyndz had brought her horse posters, that's all," Kenny admitted.

We all laughed. Poor Kenny, you just knew it had almost broken her heart to part with so much stuff!

"Well I reckon we'll only need three tables tomorrow," said Frankie, taking charge again. "One for the books and posters, that's you, Kenny and Lyndz. One for the clothes and make-up – that will be yours, Rosie and Fliss. And then I'll just need a small one for my toys."

"That's not fair!" moaned Fliss. "Everyone will notice your things because they'll be on their own."

"All right, you have the small table then," sighed Frankie.

"No, it's OK," said Fliss after a while. "I think I'd rather be with Rosie."

We all tutted. It was typical of Fliss always to want something else, just to be difficult.

With all our arrangements for the next day sorted out, we got ready for bed.

"What if no one comes," said Fliss when we were all in bed.

"Of course people will come!" snapped Kenny. "People always love buying things."

"I hope so, because if we don't raise money soon, the riding school will close for sure," I said.

"We've got to be positive!" said Frankie.

"Well *I'm* positive," said Rosie. "Positive that it's time for our midnight feast!"

We all whooped and grabbed our 'horsey' food supplies. I'd brought Wagon Wheels (you know, cowboys and all that), Fliss had brought apples, Rosie had brought Polo mints and Frankie had sliced up some carrots – all the things that horses like to eat as treats. Kenny had brought an enormous packet of chip-sticks and some Twiglets.

"What have they got to do with horses?" asked Frankie.

"The chip-sticks look a bit like hay and the Twiglets reminded me of horses' legs!" Kenny replied.

That made us all double over. We were shrieking so much, we didn't hear the knock at the door.

"Crikey, it's so noisy, I thought you'd got one of Mrs McAllister's horses in here with you!" laughed Mrs Thomas, poking her head round the door. "It's time you lot were asleep. I don't want to have to turn away crowds of people tomorrow because you're not up in time for your sale. Goodnight. Sleep tight." She closed the door and turned off the light. We waited a bit and then turned on our torches.

"I hope there *will* be a lot of people," I said.

"Bound to be" reassured Frankie. "They'll

be coming to buy all Kenny's football souvenirs. I heard them announcing it on the news."

The last thing I heard before falling asleep was Kenny trying to strangle Frankie.

The next morning was a bit grey and overcast. Not the perfect day for an outdoor sale.

"At least it's not raining," said Rosie, brightly.

We got dressed as quickly as we could and hurried downstairs. There was a lovely smell of toast wafting up from the kitchen.

"Breakfast's ready, girls!" said Mr Thomas. "I've set up the tables outside for you. What a kind man I am!"

"Thanks, Dad," said Frankie, giving him a big kiss.

We wolfed down our toast and hurried outside. The tables were just inside the garden gate. They were covered in pink material. "Wicked!" we all said.

We brought down our things from

Frankie's room and put the bags on one of the tables.

"Right, which table do you and Rosie want, Fliss?" Frankie asked her. If Fliss chose first, she couldn't complain later. She chose the one nearest the gate.

"Right then, Lyndz and Kenny, you put your things here and I'll have this small table," Frankie commanded.

Kenny and I pulled out our posters and magazines. I took out the Blu-Tack I'd brought with me and stuck some of my posters round the front of the table. Kenny did the same with some of hers. Then we arranged the magazines on top. It actually looked very good.

"What should we charge?" I asked Kenny.

"£1 a poster, 50p a magazine," she replied.

"Don't be stupid, you want to sell them don't you?" said Frankie, who had been listening. "10p and 5p sounds about right. Maybe 25p for a book."

"What about my make-up and jewellery?" asked Fliss. "Some of it was quite expensive you know."

"Yes, but you've used it," said Rosie. "I'm just going to see what people are prepared to pay. Any money is better than nothing."

"That's a good idea," said Frankie. "I might do that too."

"Hey, Frankie, it's ten o'clock!" yelled Kenny. "It's time for the grand opening."

Frankie walked solemnly to the gate. "On behalf of the Sleepover Club," she announced, "I declare this sale well and truly open!"

We all cheered and Frankie very grandly swung open the garden gate. She wasn't exactly knocked down by the rush to get in. In fact only my mum and Spike were there!

"Well, doesn't this look lovely!" Mum said.

"Do you fancy a coffee, Patsy?" Frankie's mum asked and whisked her off into the kitchen.

"Charming!" I said. "I thought she might at least have bought something first."

Spike stayed outside with us, which would have been a disaster if it hadn't been for Frankie's toy elephant. He pulled it from her table and started sucking its ears. Then he started to dig up the garden with its trunk.

"How much do you want for it?" I asked Frankie.

"£1.50?"

I looked in my purse. "I'll give you £1," I said.

"OK. Done!"

£1 was a small price to pay to keep my brother amused.

We could hear people chattering on the footpath. "Quick, more customers!" whispered Frankie.

We all rushed behind our tables and waited eagerly. But it was only Fliss's mum and her step-dad, Andy.

"There aren't many people here are there, darling?" Fliss's mum said to her. Like we really needed to hear that. Then she said, "Maybe you should have put up those posters after all."

We all looked at Fliss.

"How about a cup of coffee, Nikky?" Frankie's mum called from the kitchen.

When her mum and Andy had gone inside, we all turned on Fliss.

"What did your mum mean?" I asked.

Fliss blushed and started stuttering, "Well, I – I did put a poster on our gate and one on the tree next door. B-but Mr Watson-Wade said it made the street look untidy, so I took them down."

"So you didn't put up *any* then?" asked Kenny.

"Well, no, but I haven't seen any of yours either, so I didn't think it mattered."

"NOT MATTERED?" yelled Frankie. "Of course it mattered. How could people find out about the sale if there weren't any posters for them to read?"

"Well, where did *you* put yours then?" Fliss asked Frankie.

"On the gate, on the tree outside, on some lampposts and on a couple of bus shelters," she snapped. "I put up one in my bedroom too. But I didn't expect anyone to see *that* one."

"But we didn't see any of the others either," said Rosie quietly. "And there's definitely not one on the gate now."

Frankie went to look. "I don't believe it, they've gone!" she cried.

No one could remember seeing *any* of our posters at all. But who would have wanted to take them down? And it was obvious that someone had, because nobody was coming to even look at our things.

Our parents turned up of course, but they don't count. And as soon as she saw them, Frankie's mum took them into the kitchen anyway. Adam came and he stayed with us. But he looked so sad when no one turned up, it made us feel even worse.

In the end we bought things from each other, just to make ourselves feel better. I bought another of Frankie's toys, Fliss bought some of Rosie's old jeans (just for going to the farm in), Rosie bought some of Fliss's silver nail varnish and Frankie paid £1 for a whole pile of Kenny's football posters and programmes.

"What do *you* want those for?" Kenny asked her. "I didn't think you liked football."

"I don't," replied Frankie. "I just need some paper to make a papier mâché model with!"

"Oh no you don't!" yelled Kenny, chasing her round the garden.

We all cheered each time they ran past us. Eventually they collapsed, exhausted.

"I'll tell you what, Kenny," gasped Frankie. "You can have your stupid posters back for £1.50."

"No way!"

"Yes way – or the posters get turned to mush!"

Kenny thought about it for about ten seconds. "OK," she grumbled and handed over the money.

Just as we heard the village clock striking twelve, two figures appeared at the gate. It was the M&Ms.

"Oh dear, we haven't missed some kind of sale, have we?" asked Emma Hughes innocently.

"You really should have put up some posters to let people know you were having one," laughed Emily Berryman.

"I just hope no one is relying on you to raise money," said Queen Emma. "We'd hate to think of you letting anyone down!"

And with that the Gruesome Twosome ran cackling down the road.

"*They* must have taken our posters down!" yelled Kenny. "They're going to pay for this!"

CHAPTER SEVEN

You know what Kenny's like. She wanted to run after the M&Ms and sort them out right there and then. But the rest of us had more important things on our mind – like saving the riding school. We all felt we'd let Mrs McAllister down.

We began to pack everything away.

"What are we going to do now?" asked Frankie.

"What *can* we do?" asked Rosie glumly.

"If it hadn't been for those stupid M&Ms tearing down our posters, we'd probably have sold everything and have loads of dosh for the stables by now," shouted Kenny. She was red in the face and she looked MAD.

The sound of raised voices had brought our parents out of the kitchen. I still felt miffed they hadn't bought anything. I know we normally don't like the oldies interfering in our schemes, but this was different. They knew that the whole point of the sale was to raise money.

"That's right! Come out now when we've packed everything away!" Frankie snapped at her mum. It wasn't like her to have a go at her parents. I knew that she must be feeling as bad as me.

"Look, Frankie, I'm sorry that your sale hasn't gone well. We all are," said Mrs Thomas calmly. "But we didn't think that buying your junk was the best way for us to support you. You can have this though." She handed Frankie a tin containing loads of 50p pieces and some £1 coins.

"What's this?" asked Frankie.

"I charged everyone for coffee and

biscuits," laughed her mum. "I'm not stupid!"

"Thanks, Mum," said Frankie. "It's a start, but we need some SERIOUS money now. Any ideas?"

Everyone shook their heads. We were all idea-d out after the disappointment of the sale. Adam was getting very agitated.

"He says that you've got to think of a way to save the horses," interpreted his mother. "Look, why don't you all sleep on it and meet again at our house tomorrow afternoon. Maybe one of you will have come up with a plan by then."

"Fliss won't be home late, will she?" asked her mum anxiously. "I like her to be in bed early on a Sunday night."

Fliss blushed a shade of beetroot, but at least it made the rest of us laugh.

"Is four till six OK?" asked Rosie's mum.

Everyone agreed that it was.

As we collected all our stuff together, it felt like the end of any other sleepover. It was only when Mum was driving me and Spike home that I began to feel really miserable.

What had seemed like such a great plan had gone utterly and horribly wrong.

As soon as I got home I ran up to my room and decided that I wouldn't go down again until I'd thought of a way to save the stables. The trouble was that when I got up there, it seemed an age since breakfast – we hadn't really felt like pigging out when the sale finished after all. My stomach started to rumble and I couldn't think straight because I was so hungry. My brain was as empty as my tummy.

There was a knock at my door. It was Mum to tell me that lunch was ready. When I told her that I was going to stay there until I'd thought of a plan, she came in and sat down on my bed.

"That's an awful lot of responsibility you're putting on those shoulders, Lyndsey," she said to me. "You can't do this by yourself."

"I know, Mum," I told her. "But I've got to try."

"Well what about doing something that

involves the horses?" she suggested. "If people could see how much pleasure they give, maybe they would dig deeper in their pockets. If I were you I'd go and visit Mrs McAllister tomorrow morning and see if you can think of something together."

Mum's a genius sometimes. I gave her a hug and went down for my lunch.

When I arrived at Mr Brocklehurst's farm the next day, I was really excited because I'd been thinking about what Mum had said and I'd had an idea. But I was kind of nervous too because I didn't want to have to tell Mrs McAllister what a disaster the sale had been. I needn't have worried about it though, because when I arrived Adam and Rosie were already there with their mum.

"Hi, Lyndz!" said Rosie when she saw me. "Adam was really miserable so we came to see the horses. We've told Mrs McAllister about the sale and everything and she's been pretty cool about it. Why are *you* here?"

"I've had this idea about organising a big

Stable Fun Day with everybody getting involved with the horses. You know, with gymkhana games and things to do for children," I squealed. The more I thought about it, the better the idea became.

"Cool!" laughed Rosie.

We both danced and hugged each other. And when I told her about it, Mrs McAllister also thought it was a great idea.

We wandered across to the field to look at Bramble for a bit and then went back to the stable block where Mrs McAllister was grooming Alfie. Adam was there too and we all chatted about ideas for the Fun Day.

"I think Adam and his friends should show everybody what they can do," said Mrs McAllister, as she picked out Alfie's hoofs. "A lot of people don't know what Riding for the Disabled is all about. Would you like to show them, Adam?"

Adam nodded and smiled and pointed to Marvel.

"Yes, you can ride Marvel!" laughed Mrs McAllister.

77

"What can Lyndz do?" asked Rosie.

"Oh, I'm sure there's lots of events she can enter, don't worry!" laughed Mrs McAllister, smiling at me.

"What about my friends?" I asked. "They've got to be involved too!"

"There'll be lots for everyone to do, Lyndsey," Mrs McAllister reassured me. "The main thing is to prove that the riding school is worth saving."

It was lovely being there, thinking that we were actually going to do something to help. I felt really happy and Adam got really excited. He had some brilliant ideas too, like writing to the local newspaper asking them to come and report on the Fun Day.

When it was time to leave, Rosie's mum gave me a lift back home.

"Won't it be cool if we get this planned without the others knowing?" laughed Rosie as I got out of the car. "I can't wait to see their faces when we tell them about it."

And it *was* cool. That afternoon I arrived at Rosie's house early and helped Adam design the new posters. He'd already written the letter he was going to send to *The Leicester Mercury*. You could tell he was really fired up about the idea.

When the others turned up they all had faces like a wet weekend. You just knew that they hadn't had any more money-making ideas. It was really difficult for me and Rosie to keep straight faces. We wanted to burst out and tell them about the Fun Day straight away. But we'd agreed that we should make them sweat a bit first. Cruel or what!

"It's no good!" moaned Fliss. "We've tried our best. Maybe we're just too young for all this."

"Don't be so wet, Fliss," yelled Kenny. "Our ideas are as good as anyone else's."

"It's just that we don't have any," said Frankie sadly.

Rosie and I couldn't stand it any more. Rosie nudged Adam, who was doubled up with laughter himself.

"I don't see what's so funny!" snapped Fliss.

Adam handed them a copy of the new poster:

Help prevent the closure of
McAllister's Riding School

STABLE FUN DAY

Come and have fun with
the horses
Fun for all the family
Events for all abilities
at
Brocklehurst's Farm
Crofter's Lane
Little Wearing
Near Cuddington

Sunday 27th September
10 am - 2 pm

Admission: £3 per adult, £1.50 per child

It was wicked watching their faces as they read the poster.

"This is brilliant!" gasped Frankie. "Who thought of it?"

"Lyndz," beamed Rosie.

I blushed when she said that. I couldn't believe that the Fun Day had been my idea.

"Where are we going to put the posters so the Gruesome Twosome can't sabotage this idea as well?" asked Kenny.

"The M&Ms needn't know we're involved," I said. "Frankie's address was on the other poster, which sort of gave the game away. If the M&Ms ask, we'll just pretend we don't know anything about it. AND we'll keep an eye on the posters we do put up."

"How exactly are we going to be involved?" asked Fliss. "I won't have to ride anything will I?"

"Nobody has to get on a horse if they don't want to," Rosie reassured her. "There'll be lots of ways for us to help. We thought we could take photographs of children sitting on the horses and charge for them."

"But we're hopeless with cameras!" said Frankie.

"Yes, I know!" admitted Rosie. "Mum said she'd take the photographs if we wanted, but I don't know whether we should let the oldies get involved. You know how they take over."

We all nodded.

"I suppose if people are paying money though, they'll want a decent photo and not one of our pathetic efforts," reasoned Frankie. "Besides, we weren't very successful with the sale we organised by ourselves were we?"

We all had to admit that this was true.

"Well, maybe we could let them get involved, just a little," Rosie said. "And one of us could collect the money for the photographs, so we'd still have some control over things."

We spent the rest of the afternoon planning all the things we could do at the Fun Day. Apart from Fliss, who spent most of *her* time planning what she was going to wear!

We took some posters away with us. But

this time we told each other exactly where we were going to put them up. That way we could keep an eye on them.

We were all pretty excited about the Stable Fun Day because it felt as though we were involved in something really big and important. Even Fliss was excited, but I think that was because Adam had told her that a photographer from *The Leicester Mercury* might be there. I think she thought she might be spotted and given a modelling contract or something. Well she certainly got to be on the front page, but not in quite the way she had in mind!

CHAPTER EIGHT

The next two weeks were just one mega-blur of activity. It's a wonder we found time to go to school! We put up posters all around Cuddington. AND checked them every day to make sure they were still there. The M&Ms caught us checking one, but we pretended that we were only reading it.

"Bet you're too chicken to get on a horse aren't you, Hughesy?" Kenny called out. We all started to make clucking noises and pretended to flap our wings.

"Is that Stable Fun Day something to do with you?" asked Emma Hughes, looking down her nose at us.

"Nope!" said Frankie coolly. "We were just reading the poster. We might give it a go though."

"Really?" laughed Emily Berryman in her gruff voice. "Then maybe we should go too, Em, what do you say?" She looked at her friend and they both ran away, giggling.

"What did you say that for?" asked Fliss, going very pink in the face. "We don't want any trouble with them at the Fun Day. They'll spoil everything."

"Not if I have anything to do with it!" shouted Kenny with a nasty gleam in her eye.

But to be honest, we just didn't have time to start worrying about the M&Ms – we had far too much to worry about already!

Adam had got a reply from *The Leicester Mercury* saying that they would be sending a reporter and photographer to cover the Fun Day. And there'd been a couple of mentions of it in the paper already, which was cool. We jumped up and down like monkeys when we read those. But then we started to panic because we'd feel pretty stupid if no one turned up.

As we were trying to show everybody what a great place the riding school was, we had to think of lots of fun things to do. So, as well as gymkhana games, there had to be lots of activities for people who couldn't ride.

We'd agreed that Rosie's mum could take the photographs, then Frankie's parents said they would sell refreshments. That was OK because we thought we'd get bored making tea all day, but when my mum wanted to get involved too it looked as though our parents were going to hijack the day. But Mum is quite laid-back about stuff and said she'd just help where she could, so we agreed that she could have a go at face-painting. Kenny's mum helped us out by persuading local shops to donate prizes for some of the competitions and for a raffle, so that was cool.

I am sure you are wondering what *we* were going to do. Well, Rosie was going to help her mum, Frankie was going to face-paint with mine, and Fliss said that she'd organise the raffle. Kenny thought all those things sounded a bit girlie, so Mrs McAllister said she could help with the gymkhana games. And me? Well, I was actually going to *enter* a couple of the games on Bramble.

I hadn't done anything like that before but fortunately Bramble was an old hand. She's always being entered in gymkhanas so she knew all about stopping and starting and taking corners really tightly. I had to learn everything – including flying dismounts, where you have to leap off while the pony's still moving. Crazy! I wasn't too good at vaulting back on again, though. After a few tumbles, Mrs McAllister suggested that I should enter the sack race and the egg-and-spoon race. Once I'd dismounted in those events, I didn't have to get back on again!

I spent ages riding Bramble across the field so I knew exactly where I would have to turn her and dismount. Then I was like a loony, practising jumping about in a sack and running with an egg balanced on a spoon. And if you've ever done that on sports day, you'll know it's not so easy. Imagine doing it whilst you're leading a pony as well! Mega-crazy!

I had been looking forward to the Fun Day like anything, but when it arrived I was really nervous. I got to the farm early to get Bramble ready. It looked really cool, with flags and garlands everywhere – Mrs McAllister must have put them up the night before. The gymkhana games were being held in one of Mr Brocklehurst's fields and a few stalls had been set up in the practice ring. One of the stables at the riding school, which hadn't been damaged by the fire, was going to be used for refreshments. It had electricity so Mr and Mrs Thomas could boil up lots of water for hot drinks.

When I arrived Bramble was still in the field, so I went to catch her and then took her back to the stable block and gave her a good grooming. It was hard work, but after a while her coat was gleaming! I tacked her up, and then waited for Mrs McAllister to check her over.

"Now remember, Lyndsey, it's not about winning, it's about having fun!" she said, as she tightened Bramble's girth.

I smiled at her, but my stomach was doing somersaults.

"You might as well ride over to the field now," said Mrs McAllister. "Adam and his friends are about to perform in the opening demonstration, then it's your races!"

Once I'd mounted Bramble, I felt a lot calmer. Until, that was, Kenny, Frankie and Rosie came flying towards us.

"Hiya, Lyndz!" they yelled. "Isn't this cool?"

"Are you ready for your races?" asked Frankie.

"I think so," I mumbled.

"Don't worry, you'll thrash them!" Rosie reassured me.

"And I can always help out, if you know what I mean!" laughed Kenny.

"WHOA!" I brought Bramble to a halt. "If I

win I want it to be because I was the best, not because you cheated for me, Kenny!"

"All right, all right!" shouted Kenny. "Don't get your frillies in a flap! I won't help you at all. Promise!"

"Walk on!" I urged Bramble forward again. "Sorry," I told the others. "I'm just a bit nervous!"

As we got close to the field, we saw hundreds of people milling about.

"Wow!" exclaimed Rosie. "Look at those crowds!"

Suddenly there was a blast on a trumpet and a crashing of cymbals and we could see Adam and his friends being led into the field on their horses. Adam and Marvel were at the front. Everybody whooped and cheered and Adam had just the biggest grin on his face.

Looking round at the faces in the crowd, you could tell that everyone was amazed how well someone with cerebral palsy could cope with riding. But, better than that, they could see how much Adam and his friends were enjoying it. Frankie had rushed to grab a tin for collecting donations, and as she worked through the crowd everybody emptied their pockets of change. It was brilliant – and the day had only just started!

"Hey, Lyndz! Over here!" It was Fliss. She was done up like Marge Simpson.

"Oh… hi!" I spluttered. I was almost speechless.

"Isn't it brilliant that so many people have turned up!" she shouted up to me. "Have you seen the photographer from *The Mercury* anywhere? I thought he might want to take a picture of me."

"What, for their Horror Corner?" asked Kenny, who had sneaked up behind her.

"Ha, ha, ha!" snapped Fliss. "I wanted to look my best, that's all!"

Rosie came rushing up. "Does anyone want their photograph taken on Alfie?" she asked. "Mum wants to have a few practice shots before she starts charging anyone!"

"There you go, Fliss, the camera beckons!" I laughed.

"But I don't want to go on a horse!" she yelled.

"Alfie's as gentle as a baby!" I laughed. "Besides, if the photographer from *The Mercury* sees you, he might come and take a few pictures too!"

"Do you think so?" Fliss asked.

"We *know* so," said Kenny, rolling her eyes. "Anyway, Lyndz, I came to tell you that it's time to go into the field. The sack race is starting in two minutes."

I trotted towards the field on Bramble with Kenny running beside me. Fliss and Rosie went to the corner of the other field, where Mrs Cartwright was standing with Alfie and her Polaroid camera.

The sack race was only a fun event and I knew the other three girls who were competing. They were all friendly, so we laughed and pulled faces at each other as Mrs McAllister explained the rules to us.

As I rode over to the starting line, I could hear Kenny and Frankie shouting, "Come on, Lyndz! You can do it!"

I tried to blank everything out of my mind and concentrated on keeping Bramble totally still as we waited behind the line.

When Mrs McAllister lowered her flag, I yelled, "Come on, Bramble! Go, girl!" And we flew to the other end of the field.

I couldn't really see what anyone else was doing, but I knew that we had to do a really tight turn to get back to the centre line. I felt like I was flying. It was wicked! When I could see the centre line approaching, I prepared myself and did the most perfect flying dismount you've ever seen. I was way in front of the others.

"Come on, girl, we've got this won!" I laughed to Bramble.

I was just about to leap into my sack when I heard screaming. I know that I shouldn't have been distracted, but I recognised the scream. It was Fliss. I looked across to the other field and saw that Alfie had broken free and was galloping away. Poor Fliss was slumped across his neck, clinging on for all she was worth.

CHAPTER NINE

OK, so what would you have done? Gone on to win the race, or helped your friend? Yeah right, so a rosette is that important! I dropped my sack, urged Bramble forward and vaulted on to her. And for once I actually made it!

"Come on, girl!" I told her. "This is more important than any sack race!"

There was a gate in the corner of the field. "Kenny, open the gate!" I yelled.

She ran to where I was pointing, undid the catch and pushed the gate open. "Do you know what you're doing?" she shouted to me.

Kenny actually said that! Kenny, the girl who always rushes into things without blinking an eye and thinks about them afterwards!

"I'm not sure," I called back to her. "But I've got to help Fliss!"

I could see Alfie heading towards the bottom end of the field. I couldn't believe that Fliss was still managing to cling on to him. But they were heading for disaster: there were fences on all sides of the field, and I knew that if Alfie was really spooked he might try to jump over one of them. Fliss wouldn't stand a chance then. I urged Bramble towards them as fast as she could go.

"Hang on, Fliss!" I shouted.

Fliss just screamed.

"Try not to scream, Fliss, that'll scare him even more!" I shouted. "Try talking calmly to him."

I could hear Fliss whimpering. Of all the people to be sitting on Alfie when he decided to take off, it had to be Fliss! But I wondered why he'd done it in the first place.

Alfie was usually so calm. Something must have really frightened him to make him bolt like that. *And* he'd been tied up.

"Sit firm in the saddle, Fliss!" I called. "Put all your weight there, and hang on!"

It would have been just my luck for her to fall off as soon as I'd said that. But she didn't, she hung on in there.

I was almost level with them now, and it looked as though Alfie wasn't going to jump over the fence after all. He was slowing down and cantering around the edge of the field. I didn't really know what to do. I didn't want Bramble to get frightened as well; I just wanted to make sure that Alfie was calming down and that Fliss was safe.

I was very relieved when I heard another horse thundering towards us. It was Mrs McAllister on Marvel.

"Whoa, boy!" she said in her quiet, firm voice. She rode alongside Alfie whilst Bramble and I stayed where we were.

When Alfie had slowed down to a walk, she said to Fliss, "Sit tight, I'm going to take his reins."

Fliss stayed where she was. She had been holding on to Alfie's reins as well as his mane, but hadn't known what to do with them. To be honest with you, if the same thing had happened to me, I don't think that I would have been able to stop Alfie either. Mrs McAllister grabbed hold of the loose reins in one hand and gradually circled Alfie round to a stop.

I leapt down from Bramble, and Frankie, Kenny and Rosie came hurtling across the field towards us.

"Are you all right, Fliss!" asked Frankie and Rosie together.

"Wow! That was so cool!" panted Kenny. "You were brill, Fliss, hanging on like that. It was better than a Gladiator challenge! Awesome!"

Mrs McAllister dismounted and asked me to hold Alfie and Marvel, then she went to help Fliss dismount. "That was certainly some riding display!" she said. "I'd say you have a natural talent for this. Have you ever thought of taking it up?"

The rest of us screamed with laughter. I know it sounds awful when Fliss had just gone through such a terrible ordeal and everything, but it was sort of a release after all the excitement. Poor Fliss didn't know whether to laugh or to carry on crying – so she did both!

"Fliss is scared of horses!" I explained.

"In that case you did exceptionally well!" said Mrs McAllister squeezing her shoulder.

We all stopped laughing. The Fun Day would have been a Pretty Miserable Day if Fliss had fallen off and hurt herself. She could have had a terrible accident. It made me go all hot and cold just thinking about it.

"You were really brave, Fliss. Well cool!" I said.

"Yeah, wicked!" said the others.

"Was I?" asked Fliss. She stopped crying and looked up at us. You could tell she was thrilled that we were all praising her. But at the same time, the rest of us knew that she'd be milking this for weeks.

"It just goes to show why you must *always* wear a riding hat when you're on a horse," said Mrs McAllister. "I think I'll have to stop any more children having their photographs taken on the horses and ponies. It's not worth the risk of this happening again."

I was still holding Alfie and Marvel. Mrs McAllister took their reins from me and said, "Round up Bramble, Lyndsey, then we can walk back to the stables. OK, Fliss?"

Fliss nodded and looked all pale and pathetic. The rest of us looked at each other and rolled our eyes, but even we couldn't have a go at her when she'd just had such a terrifying experience.

Bramble was standing quietly, wondering what all the fuss was about. I gathered her reins and followed the others back to the stables. When we got there everybody crowded round us. They wanted to know what had happened and whether Fliss was all right. Even the photographer from *The Mercury* wanted a picture of her, so she was well chuffed about that. He took my photograph too, but I don't know why, just using up film I suppose.

Bramble, Marvel and Alfie loved the attention too. They were patted and stroked and just lapped it all up.

"What I can't understand," said Mrs McAllister thoughtfully, "is how Alfie got in that state in the first place. He's never bolted before. And wasn't he tied up anyway?"

Just then I spotted the M&Ms hanging around, they looked kind of embarrassed.

"I think I've found some people who'll be able to tell you," I said glancing in their direction.

Mrs McAllister took in their guilty-looking faces in a flash and stormed over. "I'd like a word with you, girls," she snapped crossly.

The M&Ms looked terrified as they followed her sheepishly into the stable office.

We tried to sneak up to listen, but I was called for the egg-and-spoon race. To be honest, I didn't feel like competing in another event. But I'd entered and I suppose I still wanted to win a rosette. But Bramble and I were both tired after our rescue mission and we had a disastrous race. I timed my dismount wrong and nearly took a tumble, then I dropped my egg *three* times. Nightmare! It was no surprise when we came in last.

Mrs McAllister had reappeared by the time we'd finished. She was a bit red in the face. The M&Ms were *bright* red and had both been crying. Mrs McAllister ignored them and handed out the rosettes for the sack race and the egg-and-spoon race.

"Never mind, Bramble. Maybe we'll get one next time!" I said as I stroked her muzzle.

"And there's a special rosette here for bravery." Mrs McAllister's voice suddenly caught my attention. "Through the stupidity of various individuals, one of my horses was frightened and ran off with an inexperienced rider on its back. I would just like to stress that this is NOT a common occurrence at my riding school." Everybody laughed. "Lyndsey Collins who was leading the sack race at the time, saw her young friend in difficulties and wasted no time in going to her assistance. She did everything absolutely right, so I would like to award this rosette to Lyndsey Collins and Bramble."

Everybody cheered and clapped like mad. I was embarrassed and thrilled to bits all at the same time, especially when I could hear my crazy friends shouting, "Way to go, Lyndz!"

That was the best bit of the Fun Day for me, but the rest of it was pretty cool too. Everybody seemed to be enjoying themselves, Fliss most of all. People kept stopping her and asking how she was. She just revelled in it and I swear that she developed a limp as the day wore on! The photographer from *The Mercury* took loads more pictures. Fliss tried her best to get in all of them, but the rest of us muscled in on quite a few too!

By the time the Fun Day ended, we were all exhausted. But we hung about as our parents counted up the money. There were huge piles of coins and bundles of notes.

"Wow, we must have raised enough to save the stables now!" squealed Rosie when she saw it all.

Do you know how much we made? Over £400. Our parents kept telling us how brilliant it was, but it wasn't thousands of pounds was it? And that's what Mrs McAllister said she needed to rebuild the stables. All our efforts looked to have been for nothing. No rosette could make up for *that* disappointment.

None of us could have expected what happened next though. And it was certainly a shock to Fliss when she saw her photograph splashed over the front page of *The Mercury* the next day.

CHAPTER TEN

We didn't actually see the paper until the afternoon, but everybody had been talking about the Fun Day at school. It was amazing how many of our class had been there. They all told Fliss how brave she was, which made the rest of us do our 'being sick' impressions, and a few of them told me that I was brave too, which was pretty cool.

The only people who didn't mention the Fun Day were the M&Ms. Mrs McAllister had found out that *they* had untied Alfie whilst Rosie and her mum were getting Fliss ready for having her photograph taken. Then two dogs had begun to fight. And if there's one thing that Alfie's scared of it's dogs. Their snarling must have terrified him and he'd taken off with Fliss on his back.

Mrs McAllister must have bawled the M&Ms out good and proper for the part they'd played in the drama, because they didn't even *look* at us all day.

So we had a pretty cool day at school, and when I got home it got even better. As soon as I got through the door, Mum handed me *The Mercury*. There on the front page was Fliss! But she wasn't looking pretty in all her finery. She was looking like a witch: screaming her head off, with her eyes bulging as she clung on to Alfie. That was one terrific photograph! The caption underneath read: *Brave Felicity Sidebotham clings to a runaway horse during the Fun Day to save McAllister's Riding School.*

"Oh dear," I said to Mum, "that's not exactly good publicity, is it? It sounds as though the whole day was a disaster."

"Turn over," Mum said.

Page two was covered with a whole load of photographs of the Fun Day. There was even one of me with the caption: *Hero of the hour, Lyndsey Collins, who rescued her friend!*

"Coo-el!" I laughed.

On page three there was a report about the Fun Day and why we had organised it. It said: *What a pity it would be if such a vital part of the community was forced to close due to lack of funds.*

At the bottom of the page it said in big letters: *SAVE THE STABLES.* Underneath there was a form to fill in if you wanted to send a donation.

"*The Mercury* is running a campaign for the stables!" I shouted, jumping up and down. "They've got to be saved now haven't they, Mum?"

"I think they probably have, yes!" Mum laughed.

I was still leaping about with excitement when the phone rang.

"Lyndz, Lyndz, have you seen the paper?" It was Frankie. "Isn't it cool? And to think we started it all off!"

No sooner had I got off the phone to Frankie when Kenny rang. "Was that Frankie on the phone? I thought it would be. Isn't it brill? We did it, girl, we saved the stables!"

"We haven't saved them yet!" I laughed. "In fact *we* haven't saved them at all. If anyone's going to save them, it's *The Mercury*."

"Yes, but we *thought* of the Fun Day didn't we? They just took over."

Kenny was right, but the paper could reach a lot more people than we ever could. That's exactly what Rosie had to say when I called her.

"Adam's unbearable!" she laughed. "He keeps telling me that the campaign in *The Mercury* was his idea."

"It doesn't really matter whose idea it was," I said. "As long as it works."

The only person who hadn't rung me was Fliss. So I rang her.

"Isn't it *awful*!" she said when she picked up the phone.

"What?" I asked.

"Isn't my photograph awful!" she said. She sounded really cross. "You'd think they could have used one of the nice ones. They took enough of me!"

"They probably used it for dramatic effect," I told her. "Besides it'll probably boost funds for the campaign. Isn't that a great idea?"

"Yeah, great," Fliss said. "Did I really look that awful, Lyndz?"

What was Fliss like? We had one of our greatest triumphs staring us in the face and all Fliss was bothered about was some crummy photo.

"No, you looked great, Fliss, honestly," I told her.

All week *The Mercury* gave details of how much money people had sent in for the Save the Stables campaign. It seemed a lot, but I still wasn't sure that there was going to be enough. I mean, Mrs McAllister had said that she needed a few thousand pounds to rebuild the stables, and that's an awful lot of money. It would mean everyone who reads *The Mercury* sending in a pound each.

On the Friday after the Fun Day, the rest of the Sleepover Club came round to my house after school. As soon as we piled through the front door we were greeted by my mum. At least we assumed it was my mum. We couldn't see her face because she had a copy of *The Mercury* right in front of it. I know, I know – seriously weird. But the headlines just about stopped us in our tracks: *LOCAL BUSINESSWOMAN SAVES RIDING SCHOOL.*

We all made a grab for the paper.

"Hey, watch it!" laughed Mum. "Let me put it on the table so you can all read it."

Local businesswoman, Sita Chandri, proprietor of Sita's Spices, has agreed to contribute what is needed to rebuild the stable block at McAllister's Riding School. The stables were recently almost destroyed by fire, and The Mercury *has been prominent in running a campaign to prevent their closure due to lack of funds. Mrs Chandri says, 'The spirit of community is very important to me. I felt that I wanted to give something back to the community which has supported me in my business ventures. Paying for the restoration of the stables seemed to be the perfect way to do that.'*

"Way to go, Sita!" shouted Kenny.

We all screamed and hugged each other. It was our idea that had sparked off the whole thing. If we hadn't had our disaster of a sale, we would never have thought about the Fun Day. And if we hadn't had the Fun Day, *The Mercury* would never have got involved and Mrs Chandri might not even have known that the riding school *needed* saving. Wicked!

So that's it, for once we have a happy ending! I'm glad it's all worked out, for Adam's sake as much as mine: he loves the horses almost as much as I do.

*

Well, we're finally at the stables. It seems to have taken us ages to get here, doesn't it? Look, Frankie and Rosie are waving at us – what are they like! And Kenny's behaving like a wild animal, as usual. That must be Fliss over there. What is she wearing? Come on, let's find out what they're up to and see if they've any more crazy schemes planned!

Sleepover in Spain

((Collins

🏰 *An imprint of* HarperCollins*Publishers*

CHAPTER ONE

Hiya, I'm back! It's me, Frankie, remember? I thought it was about time we had a chat 'cos it's been *ages* since I last talked to you. And I've got *loads* to tell you.

You haven't forgotten us, have you? There's me and my best mate Kenny, and Fliss and Rosie and Lyndz – the Sleepover Club. We've been having sleepovers for months now, and we always have a great laugh. So we were a bit shocked when Kenny said what she did. I mean, you know Kenny – she likes to stir things a bit. But this time what she said *really* made us sit up.

Anyway, it all started one afternoon at school. We were making models of horses out of clay (after our horsey sleepover, we're all nuts about horses now), so, of course, there was clay everywhere. Even Fliss was covered in it, and she's the neatest person in the known universe. She even gets her mum to iron her knickers!

"Hey, look!" Kenny stuck a lump of clay on the end of her nose, and grinned at the rest of us. "Pinocchio!"

"Thanks a lot, Kenny!" Fliss snapped, yanking it off her. "That's supposed to be my horse's tail!"

"All right, how about this then?" Kenny started sticking tiny bits of clay all over her face. "Look, it's Emma Hughes!"

We all fell about laughing. Emma's been off school with chickenpox, so her best mate Emily Berryman's had to hang out with dozy Alana 'Banana' Palmer instead. You remember Emma and Emily, otherwise known as the M&Ms, don't you? They're our Number One Enemies. Alana Banana's sort of our enemy too, but she hasn't got any brains so we don't worry about her that much.

"OK," I said, squinting down at my model. "Be honest, you lot. I can take it. Does this look like a horse to you or not?"

"Nope," said Lyndz.

"No way," said Fliss.

"No chance," Rosie added.

"It looks more like a giraffe," Kenny remarked.

"Oh, great," I said crossly, crushing my model flat. "Don't hold back, will you?"

"Your horse looks like it's been run over by a steamroller, Frankie," Mrs Weaver said, coming towards us. She raised her eye-brows at the squashed heap of clay in front of me. "What have you been doing for the last hour?"

"Sorry, Miss," I said quickly. "I just couldn't get it right." As my grandma always says, if at first you don't succeed – give up.

Mrs Weaver glanced at the clock. "Well, you've got about ten seconds left before we tidy up, so it's not worth starting again." Then she looked at us. We were all wearing overalls, but our hands were caked in clay, plus Lyndz had some in her hair and Kenny still had bits stuck on her face. "I think you'd better go and clean yourselves up too."

We lobbed our leftover clay into the clay bin, and ran for the sink in the corner. Fliss got there first.

"Ow! Stop pushing!" she complained, as we all tried to elbow our way in front of her.

"Hurry up or I'll shove a lump of clay down your neck!" Kenny warned.

Fliss jumped round, looking alarmed, and Kenny dodged smartly in front of her and began washing her hands.

"Oh, very funny!" Fliss sniffed.

"At least it wasn't ice cubes this time!" I pointed out, and we all cracked up, even Fliss. We hadn't forgotten about the sleepover when we'd tried to make a crazy video to send to *You've Been Framed*. It certainly starred the Sleepover Club, but not *quite* the way we had intended! The

10

oldies hadn't forgotten it either, they *still* went on about it sometimes.

"So what exciting plans have you got for the sleepover at yours tonight, Rosie?" Lyndz asked.

"Well, I thought we could have a fashion show," Rosie suggested eagerly.

And that's when Kenny dropped her bombshell.

"Bor-*ing*!" she said immediately. The rest of us are really into clothes, but Kenny thinks dressing up means wearing her Leicester City football strip. With boots. "Can't we do something else?"

"Like what?" Rosie asked, looking offended. You know how prickly she can be sometimes.

Kenny shrugged. "I dunno... Something *different*. We always seem to do the same old things at sleepovers these days."

We all stared at her with our mouths open.

"Are you saying our sleepovers are *no fun* any more?" Fliss gasped, outraged.

"Nah, 'course not!" Kenny reached for a

paper towel. "Sleepovers are still *cool*! It'd just be even cooler if we did something different sometimes."

"Like what?" I asked. "And don't say we could play football."

"Well, why not?" Kenny said, and the rest of us groaned loudly. "OK, but what about having a sleepover somewhere else? We only ever go to each other's houses."

"What's wrong with coming to my house tonight?" Rosie began indignantly.

"Nothing, Rosie-posie!" Kenny interrupted, flicking some water at her. It was a great shot. It hit Rosie right in the eye, and she squealed. "But don't you remember what a brilliant time we had when we slept over at the museum?"

We had to admit, she had a point.

"Well, what did you have in mind?" I asked. "A sleepover in Sainsbury's, or what?"

"Ha ha, very funny, Francesca," Kenny began, trying to annoy me by using my full name, but right at that moment Mrs Weaver yelled over the noise: "Everyone in their

12

seats now, please! I've got something very important to tell you."

We all scuttled back to our seats in silence. Kenny's remark had kind of thrown everyone, including me. *Did* we always do the same things at our sleepovers? Well, maybe we did, but we still had a great time. At least, I thought we did... No, I *knew* we did. If Kenny found them boring, it was *her* problem.

Mrs Weaver was waiting impatiently, glaring at Ryan Scott and Danny McCloud who were still chucking bits of clay at each other.

"Right, I want to tell you about a rather exciting trip that the school has arranged for this year group," she said, picking up a pile of papers from her desk. "And I have a letter for you to take home to your parents explaining all about it."

Nobody looked very thrilled. Have you ever noticed that what teachers think is exciting and what *we* think is exciting are never the same thing?

"The trip will be to the Costa Brava in

Spain for one week," Mrs Weaver went on.

There was a moment's breathless silence, and then the whole classroom erupted.

"A trip to *Spain*!" Fliss squealed. "That'll be brilliant!"

"I'm going!" Kenny said in a determined voice. "I don't care what I have to do to get my parents to say yes. I'll even be nice to Molly the Monster, sister from Hell, if I have to!"

"I reckon my mum'll let me go." Lyndz beamed all over her face. "Are you up for it, Frankie?"

"Are you kidding?" I gasped. My mum and dad are really boring when it comes to holidays. All we ever do is go to Scotland, or visit my gran in Nottingham or my grandad in Wales. Really interesting and exotic – not! "I've never been abroad before, and I really want to go!"

Suddenly Kenny bounced out of her seat with excitement. "Hey, we'll be able to have a sleepover in Spain! That'll be even *more* cool than the sleepover at the museum!"

Well, that just about did it. We were

almost wetting ourselves with excitement. Well, not quite all of us. Rosie wasn't looking very thrilled. In fact, she'd turned a funny pea-green colour.

"What's biting you, Rosie?" I asked.

"Kenny, will you sit down, please!" Mrs Weaver called. "And be quiet, everyone, so I can give you some more information about the trip before the home bell."

We all stared hard at Rosie, but we didn't get a chance to find out what the problem was because Mrs Weaver was giving us one of her looks.

"We're lucky because we've managed to book places at a very special holiday complex," she continued. "It has a swimming pool, all the usual activities, and it's right on the Costa Brava coast near the beach. But what makes this place different is that it's also an exchange centre where school children can come from all over Europe to meet each other…"

Mrs Weaver went droning on about how this was a great chance for us to make friends with kids from other European countries and learn all about each other's cultures and languages etc, etc, but nobody was listening. We were all too busy grinning at each other and making thumbs-up signs. It sounded totally brilliant. Spain, sun, sea, sand and the Sleepover Club! It was an ace combination. So I just couldn't understand why Rosie looked like someone was forcing her to spend a wet weekend in Birmingham with the M&Ms.

"Unfortunately, places are strictly limited, and only fifteen of you will be able to go." Mrs Weaver added, handing round the letters as the bell rang. "So if you're interested, you'd better bring your consent forms and the deposit to me first thing on Monday morning. Have a good weekend."

"What about you, Rosie?" Fliss asked anxiously as we picked up our bags. "You *are* going to come, aren't you?"

"'*Course* she is!" Kenny interrupted, flinging her arm round Rosie's shoulders. "We can't have a sleepover in Spain unless we're all there, can we?"

Rosie looked even more miserable. "I don't think I'll be able to. There's no way my mum can afford it."

We glanced at each other in horror. It just wouldn't be the same if we didn't *all* go.

"Well, what about your dad?" Kenny suggested. "You're always moaning about how he keeps going off on holiday with his girlfriend, even though he's promised to take you. I bet he'd be willing to pay for it."

"I don't want to ask him," Rosie muttered, and she turned and hurried out of the classroom before any of us could stop her.

"Well, that's going to ruin everything," I said angrily. Of course, the rest of us could still go, but we wouldn't be able to have a proper sleepover without Rosie, would we?

"Maybe we can talk her into asking her dad at the sleepover tonight," Lyndz suggested, and we all nodded. We had to do something, and fast, otherwise our dream of a sleepover in Spain would be over before it had even started.

CHAPTER TWO

"Mum!" I yelled as soon as I got home. "Can I go to Spain?"

My mum was working on the computer in her study, and she raised her eyebrows as I charged in, waving the letter.

"Did you say *Spain*, Frankie?"

"Yeah, there's a school trip to the Costa Brava!" I gave her the letter, and hopped impatiently from one foot to the other while she read it. "So, can I go?"

"Well, it does look quite interesting," my mum said thoughtfully. "It says here you'll get the chance to meet other kids from all over Europe, and learn about each other's cultures."

"Yeah, yeah, yeah," I muttered. Bor-*ing*! That wasn't what I was interested in. "What d'you reckon then, Mum? Can I go?"

My mum looked at me over the top of her glasses. "I suppose so, if your dad agrees."

"*Yes*!" I gave her a big hug. "Thanks, Mum!"

"What about the others? Are they going too?"

"Yep." I didn't say anything about Rosie getting her knickers in a twist, because I was pretty sure we'd be able to talk her into asking her dad for the money.

"The poor old Spanish don't know what they're letting themselves in for," my mum remarked, turning back to the computer.

I rushed out into the hall, grabbed the phone and punched in Kenny's number. I'd be seeing her in an hour or two at Rosie's, but I couldn't wait that long to break my good news.

"Hello?"

It sounded like Kenny at the other end of the line, so I started singing loudly: "*Oh, this year I'm off to sunny Spain! Y viva España!*"

There was a moment's silence.

"I think it's Kenny you want to talk to," Molly the Monster said in a freezing tone. I heard her slam the receiver onto the table and stomp off down the hall. A few seconds later Kenny picked up the phone. She was killing herself laughing.

"What did you say to the Monster, Frankie? She's got a face on her like a sour lemon!"

"Guess what?" I yelled. "My mum says I can go on the school trip!"

"Cool!" Kenny shouted joyfully. "So can I! And Monster-Features is so green with jealousy, she looks like the Incredible Hulk! Ow! Get off me, Molly!"

I waited impatiently while Kenny and Molly had a fight at the other end of the line.

"Kenny!" I yelled at last. "Get off the phone, 'cos I want to ring Fliss!"

"I'll ring Lyndz then. Right, Molly, you're

dead!" And Kenny banged down the phone.

"Of *course* I'm going!" Fliss said when I got through to her. "And so's Lyndz, I just called her. Now get off the phone 'cos I want to ring Kenny."

While Fliss was calling Kenny, I phoned Lyndz.

"So we're all going!" Lyndz said, delighted. "Except Rosie…"

"Well, we'll just have to try and talk her into it when we go over tonight." I glanced up at the clock. "Oh, rats, I'm going to be late!"

"So am I!" said Lyndz. "See you soon!"

I raced upstairs and started chucking things into my sleepover bag. Usually I take ages packing my stuff, but tonight I was too excited to care. I couldn't believe that I was finally getting the chance to go abroad. Fliss was always going on about Tenerife and Florida and Lanzarote and all the places she'd been to, and the others had been on foreign holidays too, so sometimes I felt really left out.

"Toothbrush, diary, membership card, pyjamas, slippers," I was muttering under my breath, when my mum came in.

"Hold it right there, Frankie," she said. "Mrs Cartwright has just phoned. Rosie's not very well, so the sleepover's off."

"What?" I bounced off the bed and onto my feet. "But she was fine at school today!"

My mum shrugged and went out, leaving me feeling really suspicious. It was all just a bit too convenient that Rosie was ill when she knew we were probably going to spend the whole sleepover trying to persuade her to come to Spain with us. So I legged it downstairs and phoned Kenny.

"I know – it stinks!" Kenny said when I got through. "I bet there's nothing wrong with her. I just spoke to Fliss, and she thinks Rosie's faking it too."

"I don't get it," I said, puzzled. "What's her problem?"

"I don't know, but we're gonna find out!" Kenny said. "I reckon we should all go over there anyway, right now. Can you meet us in half an hour?"

Fliss lived the closest to Rosie, so we decided to meet at her house. The others were already there when my mum dropped me off, and we set off for Rosie's place immediately.

"I don't know why Rosie's being so weird about all this," Kenny grumbled. "Anyone'd think she didn't *want* to go to Spain!"

"There must be a reason why she doesn't want to ask her dad for the money," Lyndz pointed out. "Poor old Rosie, I feel—"

"Really sorry for her!" we all chimed in.

"We won't be able to have a proper sleepover in Spain if Rosie doesn't come," Fliss said gloomily, as we went up to the Cartwrights' front door.

"She'll come," Kenny said confidently, ringing the doorbell. "Even if we have to carry her onto the plane ourselves!"

"I really want to learn flamenco dancing," I remarked. "Do you think we'll get a chance to have a go while we're there?"

"That'd be cool!" said Fliss. "I love those

big swirly dresses the Spanish dancers wear."

"Isn't flamenco dancing difficult?" Lyndz asked.

"Get out of it!" Kenny scoffed. "All you do is clap your hands and move your feet around a bit – like this." She started clapping her hands and stamping her feet and twirling round in circles, shouting "*Olé*!"

"Watch it, Kenny!" Fliss said, looking alarmed as she twirled faster.

Kenny suddenly got dizzy, staggered and pitched head-first into one of the bushy shrubs near the front door. That cracked us all up. She was still picking leaves out of her hair when Rosie's mum opened the door.

"Oh – hello!" she said, looking dead surprised to see us. "I wasn't expecting you."

"We thought we'd come and see how Rosie is," I explained.

"Yeah, we want to find out if she can come on the school trip to Spain," Kenny said eagerly. "*We're* all going."

"Oh?" Mrs Cartwright looked surprised.

"She hasn't mentioned it to me. But if she wants to go, I'm sure her dad will be happy to pay for her."

We all looked at each other. No problem there then. So why was Rosie being so funny about it all? It was a real mystery.

"Rosie's in bed, so go right up." Mrs Cartwright ushered us in. "She's got a bad headache, so don't make too much noise, will you?"

We all went up the stairs, trying not to make too much of a racket, but it wasn't easy because there was no carpet down. Rosie's house is brilliant – it's big and it has loads of rooms, but it's in a right old state. Her dad, who's a builder, had bought the house and started doing it up, but then he'd left and gone to live with his girlfriend. He was still *supposed* to be fixing the place up, but he hadn't got very far. Rosie was always moaning about it.

We stopped outside Rosie's bedroom door, and I knocked gently. No answer.

"Maybe she's asleep," Lyndz whispered.

"No chance," Kenny snorted. "We *know* there's nothing wrong with her!" And she flung the door open.

Rosie didn't see us at first. She was dancing round the room in her teddy-bear pyjamas with a Walkman in her hand and headphones over her ears, pretending to be Posh Spice.

We all waited in the doorway with our arms folded until, eventually, Rosie turned round. When she saw us, she nearly dropped down dead with shock.

"Wh– what're you doing here?" she squeaked, pulling the headphones off.

"We've come to see our sick friend," Kenny said with heavy sarcasm. "Where is she, by the way?"

Rosie blushed. "All right," she muttered sheepishly. "I'm not really ill."

"*Big* fat hairy surprise!" Kenny snapped. "So what's going on then?"

Rosie looked down at her pink furry slippers. "I didn't want to have the sleepover because I didn't want you going on at me all night about coming to Spain."

"But what's the problem?" I asked with a frown. "Your mum says that your dad'll pay."

Rosie went even redder. "I– I– I've never been on an aeroplane before!" she stammered. "And I'm scared!"

"Is that all!" Kenny began, then shut up as I elbowed her in the ribs.

"But you said you'd been abroad!" Fliss pointed out, looking puzzled.

"We went on the ferry," Rosie mumbled miserably, "and I wasn't too keen on *that*."

"I've never been on a plane before either, Rosie," I reassured her. "So I'll probably be wetting myself too. Don't worry about it."

"And I've only done it once," Lyndz chimed in. "It's really not so bad."

"I hate the take-off, though," Fliss said with a shiver. "You know, that bit when the plane first gets off the ground and it's really noisy and you feel like you're going to be sick—"

Kenny, Lyndz and I all glared at her.

"But otherwise it's brilliant, honestly,"

Fliss said quickly.

Rosie was starting to look a bit more cheerful.

"I do want to come, really," she admitted. "I'm just nervous, that's all."

"Me and Lyndz will hold your hand," I told her. "And if you throw up, we'll throw up too, just so you don't feel embarrassed."

Rosie began to giggle. "Well, I'd better go and ring my dad then, hadn't I?"

"*Yes!*" Kenny jumped up and punched the air. "The Sleepover Club's going to Spain!"

CHAPTER THREE

"*Zanahoria*," I said, checking my Spanish dictionary again. "What d'you think that means?"

The others groaned. We were sitting on the plane, waiting to take off for the Costa Brava, along with the rest of the kids who were going. Me and Lyndz were sitting with Rosie, to give her moral support, and Kenny and Fliss were across from us. Everyone was so excited, we were totally hyper, and we were driving Mrs Weaver and Miss Simpson, the other teacher who was going with us, crazy. At the moment they were running up and down the aisle, checking that nobody had been left behind in the duty-free shop.

"Frankie, you've been driving us bananas with that dictionary for weeks now!" Kenny glared at me. "Give it a rest, will you!"

"Come on, don't be a dweeb!" I retorted. "We've got to make a bit of an effort to learn some of the language."

"Why?" Fliss asked, fastening her seat belt. "Loads of people in Spain speak English anyway."

"That's not the *point*," I sighed. "Go on, have a guess what *zanahoria* means."

"School?" Rosie suggested.

"Aeroplane?" Lyndz offered.

"An annoying twit who won't keep their big mouth shut?" Kenny asked pointedly.

"Ha ha. No, it's Spanish for carrot."

"Oh, great big fat hairy deal," Kenny retorted. "That'll be so-o-o useful."

Rosie was rummaging in the pocket on the back of the seat in front of her.

"What's this for?" she asked, holding up a paper bag.

"What do *you* think?" Kenny grinned.

"You mean they give you a *bag*?" Rosie looked horrified at the thought. "That's really embarrassing!"

"It'd be even more embarrassing if you *didn't* have one!" Fliss pointed out, and we all started giggling.

"OK," I said, flipping through my dictionary again. "Try this one. *Conejo*."

"Haven't a clue," Lyndz yawned.

"No idea," said Rosie.

"Rabbit!" I said triumphantly.

"Oh, radical," said Kenny. "So if I happen to meet a talking *conejo* on the Costa Brava, I can ask him if he wants a *zanahoria*."

"All right, girls?" Mrs Weaver stopped at our seats, looking about ten million times more stressed out than she usually does at school. "Now, are you sure you've got all your hand luggage with you?"

"Yes, Miss," we chorused. We all had our Sleepover Kit in our hand luggage, including our diaries and membership cards. Our diaries contain our biggest and most intimate sleepover secrets, so there was no way we wanted to lose *those* in a hurry.

"Good. Now I want you to be on your best behaviour at all times," Mrs Weaver went on. We could tell that she was warming up to the speech she'd given us nearly every day at school for the last few weeks. "Just remember that you're representing Great Britain while you're in Spain, and we want people to get a good impression, not only of our country, but also of our school…"

We all tried not to yawn. Kenny was pretending to listen, but she'd secretly pulled out a can of Coke from her pocket, and was trying to open it without Mrs Weaver noticing.

"…so be aware that at all times you are an ambassador for our country—

"Aargh!" Mrs Weaver screamed, and we all ducked as Kenny popped open the can, sending a shower of Coke everywhere.

"Sorry, Miss!" Kenny spluttered. "It must have got shaken up!"

Mrs Weaver looked as if she'd quite like to

grab Kenny and give *her* a good shaking.

"Just remember what I've been saying, Laura," she remarked in a threatening tone, and went off, wiping her face.

"Wow, she called me Laura!" Kenny said, passing the can round. "That means she's *really* mad."

"Now she's telling Ryan Scott off," Lyndz said. "Did you see that ginormous bar of chocolate he bought in the duty-free shop? Well, he's eaten half of it already!"

"Better lend him our sick bags," Kenny remarked. "I suppose you're well pleased Ryan's coming with us, aren't you, Fliss?"

Fliss blushed. She's had a thing about Ryan Scott for ages.

"Well, at least he's better than the M&Ms!" she retorted.

We all grinned at each other. The M&Ms were missing out on the trip because Emma Hughes had been absent when the forms were given out. Emily Berryman didn't want to go without Emma, so we were only stuck with Alana Banana. And as I said before, she doesn't really count.

Suddenly the plane started to move, and I sat up. "We're off!"

All the kids from our school cheered and started giving each other high fives as the plane taxied towards the runway. Lyndz was trying to cheer and drink Coke at the same time, so, of course, she got hiccups, and then one of the stewardesses had to bring her a glass of water.

"What's happening now?" Rosie asked nervously as a voice over the speakers told us to watch the stewardesses' demonstration carefully.

"They're going to tell us what to do if the plane goes down," Kenny said through a mouthful of chocolate.

"What!" Rosie turned pale.

"Don't get all wound up," I told her, as the nearest stewardess showed us how to put on a life jacket. "We'll be fine."

The plane came briefly to a halt at the top of the runway. There was a great roar of engines, and Rosie closed her eyes as it picked up speed.

"I want to go home," she muttered.

The plane rushed forward and then, just when we were beginning to think that it would never make it, it lifted up into the air, climbing higher and higher every minute.

"Hey, that wasn't so bad!" Rosie said, relieved. She leant across Lyndz, who was sitting by the window, and looked down. "Wow! Look at the airport, Frankie – it looks really small already."

I didn't answer. I was slumped in my seat with my eyes closed, shivering all over, and feeling as if I'd left my stomach behind on the ground when we took off.

"Hey, Frankie," Kenny called across the aisle, "what's Spanish for 'airsick'?"

"Shut it, Kenny," I muttered, feeling my tummy do five backflips in a row as the plane carried on climbing.

Even though I began to feel better when we were right up above the clouds, once you couldn't see the ground the journey was actually pretty boring. The only good bit was when the stewardesses brought round some food, but even compared to Sleepover Club standards of cooking, it didn't ta. e that great. It seemed ages until the Captain finally told us that we were coming in to land at the Spanish airport.

"We're here! We're here!" Rosie exclaimed, bouncing up and down in her seat.

"Hey, take it easy," I said, alarmed. "You don't want to rock the plane while we're landing!"

The others started to laugh.

"What's Spanish for 'dumbo', Frankie?" Fliss asked between giggles, and I chucked the dictionary at her.

Coming down was loads better than going up, and when I stepped off the aeroplane, I couldn't believe that I was actually in Spain. It was dark, so we couldn't see much, but although the air felt warmer than at home, the airport didn't look that different from the one we'd just left behind in England.

We had to wait ages to collect our bags, and Kenny got told off by Mrs Weaver for trying to ride round on the luggage carousel, then at last we all piled out of the airport and onto a minibus. But I felt a bit let down *again* because there was nothing new to see on the journey, either. Just some roads, and loads of cars.

"This is no different from Leicester!" I said in a disappointed voice to Fliss.

"I've never seen a palm tree in Leicester!" Fliss pointed out.

"OK, *except* for the palm trees."

Lyndz and Rosie fell asleep, and the rest of us could hardly keep our eyes open either, but when we arrived at the holiday complex, we all sat up and had a good look.

It was *brilliant*. The place was floodlit, so we could see that all round the grounds were blocks of dormitories where we'd be sleeping, and in the middle of them was a huge swimming pool with two water-slides and a chute, which was surrounded by loads of deck chairs. There was also a games hall, tennis courts, a bowling alley and a kind of mini funfair. Our eyes were out on stalks.

"This is *fab!*" Kenny gasped, as we all practically fell over each other in our rush to get off the coach. "We're going to have a brilliant time!"

We'd pulled up outside one of the dormitory blocks, right next to where another coach was already parked. A load of kids who looked as if they were Spanish were just climbing off and waiting for their suitcases and bags.

"Right, gather round, please," Mrs Weaver called, waving her clipboard at us as our driver started to unload the luggage. "I'm going to tell you your room numbers, so listen carefully. Lyndsey Collins, Rosie Cartwright and Felicity Sidebotham – number seven. Francesca Thomas, Laura McKenzie and Alana Palmer – number twelve…"

"We're not in the same room!" Rosie gasped, looking worried. "How're we going to have a sleepover if we're not all sleeping together?"

"Kenny and me'll just have to sneak into your room," I said.

"But we're in with dozy Alana Banana!" Kenny groaned.

"Don't worry about Alana, we'll just ignore her like we usually do—" I began. But Kenny wasn't listening.

"Hey, that girl's nicked my bag!" she yelled. And the next second she was legging it over to one of the Spanish kids who'd been waiting beside the other coach. I followed her. The girl, who was wearing a Real Madrid football shirt, was walking into the dormitory block with four other girls, and she was carrying Kenny's blue Adidas bag.

"Kenny! What on earth's going on?" Mrs Weaver hurried over as Kenny tried to yank the bag out of the girl's hands.

"That's my bag, Miss!" Kenny gasped. She was having a tug-of-war with the Spanish girl, who wouldn't let go either.

"No, it is not!" the girl snapped, glaring at Kenny. "This bag is mine!"

"Give it back!" Kenny pulled even harder.

"Er – Kenny…" Fliss hurried over to us. She had a blue Adidas bag in her hand. "I think you'll find *this* one's yours. Our coach driver's just got it out of the boot."

"You'd better apologise, Kenny," Mrs Weaver said tartly, and went off.

"Sorry," Kenny muttered to the Spanish girl, who was giving her a dirty look. So were her four friends.

"It is OK," she snapped. "Everybody know the English is stupid!" She glanced at Kenny's Leicester City football shirt. "And the football teams are terrible!"

"What!" Kenny clenched her fists. The five girls giggled and went into the dormitory block, chattering to each other in Spanish.

We all glared after them.

"What a load of stuck-up nerds!" Rosie gasped.

"Yeah, they'd better keep out of our way in future!" Kenny said furiously

But d'you know what? I had a feeling we hadn't seen the last of those girls…

CHAPTER FOUR

"Oh, this is *ace!*" I gasped, as Kenny and I went out onto the balcony and looked across the holiday camp. Although it was still quite early in the morning, the sun was already warm and the sky was blue. We could even see the sea in the distance. At last I was starting to feel that I was actually in Spain.

"Fabbo," Kenny agreed, squinting in the bright light. "Hey, did you hear Alana Banana snoring last night? She sounded like a bullfrog!"

"Don't be unkind to bullfrogs!" I laughed.

"Come on, let's grab our stuff and go to the bathroom before she wakes up."

We tiptoed back into our room, which was really small and only just about had enough room for three beds and a wardrobe. Then we collected our towels and toothbrushes and legged it, leaving Alana Banana still snoring. We were at the other end of a long corridor from Fliss, Rosie and Lyndz, so we hurried down to their room and banged on the door. They were just getting out of bed.

"Come on, lazybones!" Kenny said, sticking her head round the door. "If we get washed and dressed quick, we can go out and explore!"

"Mrs Weaver said we weren't to go anywhere before breakfast—" Fliss began, but Kenny grabbed a pillow off Rosie's bed, and lobbed it at her.

"Oh, don't be such a goody-goody, Fliss! Come on!"

Two minutes later we were all in the bathroom. There was no one else there, so we each got a shower cubicle to ourselves.

"Does anyone know what we're doing today?" Kenny called over the noise of the running water.

"Mrs Weaver said that we're going to the beach!" Rosie called back.

"Sounds ace!" I said, grabbing my towel and drying myself off. "I hope we don't see those snooty Spanish girls again though."

"Well, if we do," Kenny said grimly, "I'm gonna tell them exactly what I think of them!"

"I thought Mrs Weaver said we were supposed to be making friends with kids from other countries," Fliss pointed out.

"Yeah, but not if they're snooty, stuck-up and a pain in the neck!" Kenny retorted.

We opened the doors of our showers, and came out. Then we stopped in our tracks. The five Spanish girls were standing there in their pyjamas, holding their towels and toothbrushes, glaring at us.

Kenny was the first to recover. "Got a problem?" she asked jauntily.

The girl who'd had the Adidas bag the night before stepped forward, looking furious. "Yes, I have. You."

"*Ten cuidado*, Maria," said the tallest girl, who had long black hair in a ponytail.

"Careful, Kenny," I said at almost exactly the same moment.

Kenny and Maria ignored both of us.

"Oh yeah?" Kenny moved forward too, staring Maria right in the eye. "Well, that's just your tough luck, isn't it?"

"Cool it, Kenny," I said firmly, grabbing her arm. "Let's get out of here." And between the four of us, we managed to get her outside into the corridor.

"What did you do that for?" Kenny said crossly. "I was just about to knock her block off!"

"That's what we were worried about!" Rosie pointed out. "D'you want Mrs Weaver to go ballistic?"

Kenny suddenly started grinning from ear to ear. "Hang on a sec," she whispered, and tiptoed back into the bathroom. The Spanish girls had already gone into the showers, and Kenny moved silently along the row until she saw Maria's red pyjamas, which were hanging over one of the doors. Kenny reached up, grabbed them and chucked them straight out of the open window.

"*Ay*! *Mi pijama*!" We heard Maria yell indignantly from inside the cubicle, but we didn't wait to see what happened. We fled along the corridor back to our rooms, laughing our heads off.

"That'll show her!" Kenny giggled, as we skidded to a halt outside Fliss, Rosie and Lyndz's room. "Serves her right!"

"I see you're all up bright and early." The door of the next room opened and Mrs Weaver came out. "Breakfast in ten minutes, remember."

"Hey, that's a bit of a downer," I whispered to the others as Mrs W went off. "I didn't know she was in the room next to you lot. If we have a sleepover, she'll hear everything!"

"Yeah, that's a point," Kenny agreed. "And we definitely can't have one in our room because of Alana Banana."

"Alana's so dopey, she might not notice," Lyndz said hopefully.

"Yeah, but we'd have to listen to her snoring!" I said. "Nope, we'll just have to have the sleepover in your room, and hope Mrs Weaver doesn't catch on."

"Come on, let's get dressed, and go and grab some breakfast." Kenny headed back down the corridor towards our room. "I'm starving!"

The canteen was in a large, spacious hall next door to our dormitory block. Most of the kids from our school were already there, sitting at long tables, and so were the teachers. We collected our cereal and toast, and joined them.

"Where's Alana, Frankie?" Mrs Weaver asked with a frown.

"She's just getting up, Miss," I replied. "Well, she'd opened her eyes anyway."

We sat down and started to attack our food hungrily.

"Right, everyone, we'll be meeting at the entrance of our dormitory block in exactly half an hour," Mrs Weaver said briskly. "We've got some very exciting activities planned for you down on the beach this morning, and you'll have a chance to meet up with some of the other school children who are staying here."

Kenny groaned. "Oh, great! Like I *really* want to spend the morning with those gruesome Spanish girls!"

"I wonder if Maria got her pyjamas back!" I said with a grin.

Just at that moment Maria and her friends walked into the canteen. They clocked us straightaway, but instead of looking angry, they started giggling and pointing at us.

"Hey, what's going on?" Fliss asked. "Why're they laughing at us?"

"Who knows?" Kenny shrugged. "Just ignore them."

We soon found out why Maria and her friends were in hysterics on our way back to the dormitory block. There was a tree just

47

outside the canteen, and there were clothes hanging off some of the branches. There was a football shirt, two T-shirts, a pair of jeans and a pair of pink knickers.

"That's my best top!" Lyndz wailed.

"Those're my favourite jeans!" I yelled.

"That's my Spice Girls T-shirt!" Rosie gasped.

"And those're my knickers!" Fliss hissed in a strangled voice.

"Someone's chucked our clothes up here!" Furious, Kenny jumped up and tried to grab her football shirt, but she couldn't reach it. "And I bet I know who!"

"What *I'd* like to know is how they knew where to find our stuff in the first place," I said.

"They must have watched which rooms we went to when we left the bathroom," said Lyndz.

"Hurry up!" Fliss begged, as Kenny shinned quickly up the tree. "Before anyone comes!"

"You know what?" Kenny said through

gritted teeth as she grabbed Fliss's knickers and chucked them down to her. "This means war!"

CHAPTER FIVE

"Look at them!" Kenny whispered in my ear, disgusted. "They're laughing their stupid heads off!"

"Yeah, we've got to think of a way to get our own back!" I agreed, and Rosie, Fliss and Lyndz nodded.

We were just getting onto our minibus and the Spanish girls were getting onto their one, which was parked next to it. They were smirking at us smugly through the windows.

"I'd like to push them into the swimming pool!" Fliss muttered under her breath as we sat down. "I can't believe they threw my knickers into a tree!"

"They're gonna be sorry they messed with us," Kenny growled. "I ripped my footy shirt while I was getting it down."

We all glared at the Spanish girls, and they pulled faces at us.

"Is there a problem, girls?" Mrs Weaver asked with a frown, as she got on the bus.

"No, Miss," we all said quickly.

"Well, I hope no one's forgotten their sun cream!" Mrs Weaver said with a smile, as the driver climbed in and we moved off. "We're going to be at the beach for most of the day."

"Oh, I can't wait to get to the sea!" Fliss squealed excitedly. "I'm going to lie in the sun and get a brilliant tan!"

"You'll be lucky," Kenny retorted. "Didn't you see that list of activities Mrs W had on her clipboard? We've got to choose one to do."

"What?" Fliss asked, looking dismayed.

"Yeah, volleyball, cricket, Frisbee, surfing." Kenny ticked them off on her fingers. "Oh, and five-a-side football."

"NO!" the rest of us said loudly.

"Oh, *all right*," Kenny grumbled. "But what about surfing? That looks pretty cool."

"Hey, Fliss!" Ryan Scott called from the back seat. "You haven't forgotten your *underwear*, have you?" And he and his mate Danny McCloud fell about laughing.

Fliss turned the colour of a ripe tomato. "I could kill those girls!" she muttered.

"Oh, let's forget about them and have a good time," Lyndz suggested cheerfully. "That's why we're here, remember?"

We all got more and more excited as the minibus headed out of the holiday complex, and down to the sea. As we drove through the town, we saw loads of cafés and restaurants, and all kinds of souvenir shops.

"I hope we get a chance to do some shopping," Rosie said. "I want to buy a donkey in a straw hat!"

"How gross!" Kenny remarked. "Hey, that'd be the perfect present for Molly the Monster!"

We all leapt out of our seats at the first

glimpse of the sea. As the minibus drew to a halt, my eyes were almost falling out of my head because I'd never seen a beach like this one. It was long and winding, the sand was clean and golden, and the water was a clear, deep green. It was a whole lot better than some of the grungy beaches I'd been to in England!

"Ace!" I said happily, as we all pulled off our shoes and followed Mrs Weaver across the sand. "I hope it's chucking it down with rain back home, and the M&Ms are getting soaked!"

"Talking of the M&Ms," Rosie said in a low voice, "they'd probably get on really well with *them*!"

We all looked down the beach. Maria and her friends were a little way off with the rest of the group of Spanish kids, standing round their teacher, Miss Moreno.

"They've got it coming!" Kenny muttered, giving them the evil eye. "Nobody ruins my footy shirt and gets away with it!"

"Oh, ignore them," I said. "We don't want

them spoiling our day!"

"Yeah, Frankie's right," Lyndz agreed. "Let's just keep away from them!"

Yeah, *right*. When Mrs Weaver asked us what activities we wanted to do, we decided on surfing, and she sent us over to our instructor, who was an Australian called Jo. Guess who was already standing there with surfboards in their hands?

"G'day, girls!" said Jo, who sounded like she ought to be in *Neighbours*. "Great to meet you all. This is Maria, and this is Pilar" – she pointed to the tallest girl – "And this is Isabella, and the twins Anna and Elena."

Isabella, Anna and Elena hadn't said much so far, but they were making up for that by staring at us extra-snootily. Isabella was small and thin and had long hair in a ponytail, and Anna and Elena were taller with short, dark curly hair, although for twins they didn't look that much alike.

"Well, we're going to have a ripper time this morning, girls," Jo said cheerfully, as Kenny pulled a cross-eyed face at Maria.

"And you're all going to be great mates at the end of it!"

We all stood there silently, eyeballing each other grimly.

"Er – let's get started then." Jo looked a bit flustered as she passed us each a surfboard. "Have any of you guys ever surfed before?"

"Yes," Pilar said immediately.

"No," I said, and the Spanish girls all started grinning.

"It's cool," Kenny cut in quickly. "We'll be able to do it, no probs."

"It's not quite as easy as it might look." Jo was beginning to get even more flustered as she spotted Maria sticking her tongue out at Kenny. "But the waves here are pretty gentle, so you'll be quite safe."

"They *would* be able to surf," I muttered to Fliss, as we took off our T-shirts and shorts. "Now we're going to look right idiots next to them."

"I know," Fliss began. Then she let out a scream. "Look!"

"What's up, Fliss?" Kenny asked. "Seen a

shark?"

"That – that Isabella's got the same swimsuit on as me!" Fliss spluttered.

We all looked at Isabella, who'd just taken her shorts off. She was wearing exactly the same hot-pink bikini with white spots on as Fliss was.

"I'm not wearing this again!" Fliss grumbled, stuffing her clothes into her beach bag.

"Could be embarrassing when you're sunbathing then," Kenny remarked.

"Don't be daft," Fliss retorted, "I've brought six other swimsuits with me!"

"All ready, girls?" Jo hurried over to us. "Let's go down to the water."

Maria, Pilar and the others had already waded out into the sea, and were lying on their fronts on their surfboards, riding in on the waves.

"Hey, that's not *proper* surfing!" Kenny scoffed. "You're supposed to stand up!"

"Yeah, we can do *that*, no problem!" Rosie agreed.

Just then a really big wave came in, and all five of the Spanish girls jumped upright on their surfboards, and rode the wave into the shore like experts. We all looked at each other in dismay.

"Right, put your boards down in the water, and lie on them," Jo instructed us. "The first thing we're going to practise is paddling out."

Jo showed us how to move ourselves into the water by paddling with our arms. Then we had to turn round on the boards so that we were facing the beach, and let the waves shoot us back in. It wasn't as easy as it looked. The first big wave sent me tumbling off my board, and under the water. When I came up spluttering, Rosie, Kenny, Fliss and Lyndz were all doing the same thing, and Maria and the others were killing themselves laughing, and calling out things in Spanish, which we couldn't understand.

"Go with the wave, don't try to fight it," Jo told us. "And when you feel confident, you can start moving the board around a bit, and try coming in at an angle."

After we'd been practising for a while, we started to get pretty good, so, of course, Kenny began to get a bit cocky.

"I'm gonna stand up for this one!" she yelled, as we saw a huge wave beginning to break.

"No, Kenny!" the rest of us screamed, but she ignored us. As the wave crashed down, she jumped up on her board – and disappeared completely. She reappeared a moment later, coughing and spluttering and looking half-drowned.

"Oi, Kenny!" Maria called, helpless with laughter. "You want to do this, yes?" And she stood up on her board and surfed into the shore.

"OK, that's it!" Kenny gasped, coughing up about ten pints of sea water. "It's payback time. They're gonna get what's coming to them right now!"

CHAPTER SIX

"What're we going to do?" Lyndz asked, as we paddled over to them.

"Watch me!" Kenny replied. She went right up to Maria, who didn't see her coming because she was swimming out to catch the next wave, and tipped her off her surfboard. We all screamed with laughter, and paddled off. Jo started calling us from the beach, but we ignored her.

"Aargh!"

We all heard Fliss scream, and turned round. We were just in time to see Isabella grab hold of Fliss's board, and tip her into

59

the water with a splash.

"Right! You're dead!" Kenny yelled. "Come on, let's get them!"

We all paddled furiously towards the Spanish girls. Lyndz got there first, and pushed Elena right off her board, and Rosie lunged at Anna and tipped her off too. I headed for Pilar. I reckoned that was only fair, because she was the tallest, like I was. But I never got to her, because now Jo was *really* mad.

"STOP THAT AT ONCE!" she roared, wading out into the water. "AND GET BACK HERE RIGHT NOW!"

We all paddled sulkily back to the shore.

"What on *earth* do you think you were doing?" Jo shouted furiously at us. "You could have hurt each other!"

"That was the idea!" Kenny muttered.

After the battle of the surfboards, Jo sent us off in disgrace. Luckily Mrs Weaver didn't notice because she was teaching a group of kids to play volleyball, so we grabbed a spare Frisbee and messed about with that for a while. Then it was time for lunch.

"I reckon we got a result, anyway," Kenny said as we sat under a parasol, unpacking our sandwiches. "We knocked three of those nerds off their boards, and they only got Fliss."

"I just wish I'd got Pilar," I remarked, as I towelled my hair dry. "I reckon she's the leader of that gang, even though Maria's got the biggest mouth!"

Rosie's eyes widened. "Hey, that's just like you and Kenny!"

"What?" Kenny and I stared at her.

"Well, Pilar's really tall, and Maria likes football..." Rosie's voice trailed away.

"We're nothing *like* them!" Kenny said indignantly, and Rosie turned pink.

"I'm *not* surfing again this afternoon," Fliss said firmly. "I just want to lie here and get brown."

"I want to ring my mum," Rosie said.

"Get out of it!" Kenny scoffed. "We've only been here a day!"

"I know," Rosie looked a bit embarrassed,

"I just want to check how everyone is."

That started me thinking about my mum and dad and Pepsi, my dog, back home in Cuddington. Suddenly England seemed a very long way away.

"I haven't been away from home on my own this long before," Fliss muttered tearfully.

So there we were, munching our sandwiches, on a beautiful, hot day, watching the sea roll in, and looking like really sad cases. Even Kenny was looking a bit down. I decided it was time for some action.

"Hey, why don't we have our Spanish sleepover tonight?" I suggested.

"I thought we were going to wait till the end of the holiday," Lyndz said.

I shrugged. "So what? We can have more than one, can't we?"

Everyone nodded eagerly. Just thinking about having a sleepover made us all feel a lot more cheerful.

"We'll have to buy some food for the

midnight feast," Rosie pointed out.

"We can get that from the shop at the holiday complex, no problem," I said. "Kenny and me'll sneak over to your room tonight as soon as Alana Banana's asleep."

"What if she wakes up and sees you're gone?" Fliss asked anxiously.

Kenny shook her head. "She won't!" she said confidently. "Alana Banana's so dozy, she'd sleep through an earthquake!"

"Isn't she asleep yet?" Kenny whispered, leaning across the narrow gap between our beds, so that Alana wouldn't hear.

"Nope, I can still hear her moving around."

"She's a real pain in the neck!" Kenny groaned, flopping back onto her pillow. "Look, it's after midnight already!"

When we'd got back from the beach earlier that afternoon, we'd played tennis and gone bowling. We were both so wiped out from all the exercise and sea air, we could hardly keep our eyes open. Maybe arranging a sleepover for tonight hadn't been such a good idea...

"Ow! My nose is sore!" Kenny complained. "I think I've burnt it. Does it look red?"

"Yeah, it's glowing in the dark like Rudolf's," I told her.

"Oh, ha ha." Kenny said, then she went quiet. Somehow I managed to keep my eyes open, and as soon as I heard Alana Banana snoring, I reached over and poked Kenny.

"Ow! Wassat?" Kenny mumbled dozily.

"Alana Banana's asleep at last," I said, swinging my legs out of bed. "And so were you, by the sound of it!"

"No, I wasn't." Kenny rolled out of bed, yawning. "Come on, let's go. And don't forget the food."

I picked up the carrier bag. We'd had a Spanish thing called *tapas* for our dinner, which was brilliant. There were loads and loads of little dishes, all containing different things like olives, potato omelette, stuffed mushrooms, sausages and salads. So while we were eating we'd all been busy pocketing stuff that we could keep for our midnight feast.

We took our torches and tiptoed over to the door. Kenny pulled it open cautiously, and we looked out into the brightly-lit corridor.

"I'm going to turn the light off," Kenny whispered, "so we've got a better chance of getting away if either of the teachers hear us."

"Well, I hope we don't barge into Mrs Weaver's room by mistake!" I said anxiously. Mrs W had given us a long talk the night before about how we were not to sneak into each other's rooms at night under any circumstances. Of course, we weren't going to take any notice of *that*. We were just going to do our best not to get found out.

Kenny hurried across to the light switch on the opposite wall, and flipped it off. Immediately it went so dark, we couldn't make out our hands in front of our faces. We didn't have time to turn on our torches though, because the next moment the lights came back on.

Kenny, who was coming towards me, froze. "Someone's used one of the other switches!" she hissed. "Quick, shut the door – they might be coming this way!"

Kenny dashed back into our room, just as Pilar came round the corner. Quickly we pushed the door to, and waited, our hearts pounding. Then we looked out cautiously again, just in time to see her go into the bathroom.

"She must be going to the loo," Kenny whispered. "D'you think she saw us?"

"I don't think so." I pulled the door open. "Come on, we'd better get to the others before she comes back. Leave the light on this time, or she might get suspicious!"

We ran down the corridor to room number seven. But when I turned the handle, the door wouldn't budge.

"It won't open!" I gasped.

"What!" Kenny nearly had a fit. "They must've locked it on the inside! We'll have to knock."

"Don't be an idiot!" I hissed. "If we do that we'll wake up Mrs Weaver!"

"Well, what d'you suggest then? We've got to do *something*!" Kenny hissed back. "Pilar'll be out in a minute, and she'd just love to drop us right in it!"

Suddenly we heard the noise of a bolt being pulled back, and the door opened. Fliss was standing there, blinking at us sleepily, and we nearly knocked her over as we barged in. Rosie and Lyndz sat up in bed, yawning and rubbing their eyes.

"Sorry," Fliss said. "We fell asleep, and forgot we'd bolted the door."

"Thanks a bunch!" Kenny said. "We nearly got caught by Pilar. She's in the bathroom."

The others looked alarmed.

"Did she see you?" Rosie asked.

"Nope." Kenny shook her head. "Good job too, because she'd probably tell Mrs Weaver like a shot."

I got under the duvet at the bottom of Lyndz's bed, and Kenny got into Fliss's.

"What shall we do first?" Lyndz asked in

a low voice.

"Something quiet," Fliss begged. "I'll die if Mrs Weaver wakes up."

"We could write in our diaries," Rosie suggested. "That's pretty quiet."

"Good idea," I agreed.

"Yeah, OK, but we ought to do something *special* first," Kenny added.

"Like what?" Fliss frowned.

"Well, it's our first sleepover in a foreign country," Kenny explained, "so maybe we ought to make a speech or something."

I grinned. "Go on, then."

"OK." Kenny jumped out from under the duvet, and stood up on Fliss's bed. "Welcome to our very first *dormir sobre!*"

We all blinked.

"You what?" I said blankly.

"*Dormir sobre* – it's Spanish for sleep-over!" Kenny grinned. "I looked it up in Frankie's dictionary. Well, I looked up *sleep* and I looked up *over*, and then I just put them together!"

"Nice one!" Lyndz said, and we were all

going to applaud, but then we remembered Mrs Weaver was just next door, so luckily we didn't.

"You know what?" Kenny went on. "I reckon we should try to have a sleepover in every single country in the world – then we'd get into the *Guinness Book of Records*!"

"What, even Iceland?" Fliss shivered.

"Yeah, a sleepover in an igloo!" Rosie suggested, and we all put our hands over our mouths to stop the giggles.

We were still laughing when, without warning, the door flew open and Mrs Weaver stormed in.

CHAPTER SEVEN

Kenny was so shocked at the sight of Mrs Weaver, she fell backwards and landed on top of Fliss, who squealed.

"What on *earth* is going on in here?" Mrs Weaver said furiously, looking round at us with her worst, beady-eyed stare. "You were told not to leave your rooms at night unless you needed to go to the bathroom!"

"Yes, Miss. Sorry, Miss," we all said miserably.

Suddenly I noticed Pilar standing in the corridor, peeping in through the open door. She saw me looking at her, and grinned wickedly before walking off.

"I'm very disappointed with your behaviour," Mrs Weaver went on sternly, making us all feel about five centimetres tall. "These rules were made for a reason – we have to know exactly where everyone is in case there's a fire drill, or some other emergency."

We all sat there silently, not daring to say anything.

"Francesca and Laura, go back to your room immediately. We won't say anything more about this, but" – Mrs Weaver stared round at us, her face grim – "if it happens again, Miss Simpson and myself will have to move into the same rooms as you. Now off you go."

"That was close," Kenny muttered, as we hurried back to our room under the stern eye of Mrs Weaver. "I don't fancy bunking in with the teachers!"

"Yeah, well, maybe if Pilar hadn't dropped us in it, we'd have got away with it!" I said angrily.

Kenny's eyes widened. "You mean, Pilar *did* see us, and told Mrs Weaver?"

I nodded. "I reckon so. She was in the corridor when Mrs Weaver was bawling us out – didn't you see her?"

"No, I didn't!" Kenny clenched her fists. "The nasty little toad! Well, we'll just have to be more careful next time."

"What, you mean we're still going to try and have a sleepover?" I asked.

"'Course we are!" Kenny said in a determined voice as we entered our room, where Alana Banana was still snoring loudly. "We're not going to let Pilar and her gang get the better of us, are we?"

"Nope, I guess not," I replied. But I couldn't help wondering what Mrs Weaver would do if she caught us out of our room again at night.

"So Pilar *did* see you!" Rosie exclaimed, as we ate our breakfast the following morning.

"Yep, we reckon she dropped us right in it," Kenny said furiously, mashing her

Weetabix to a pulp. "So the question is, what're we gonna do about it?"

"Oh, never mind them," said Lyndz. "What are we going to do about our sleepover?"

"Well, I think we ought to wait a few days and then try again," Kenny said.

Fliss turned pale. "What if we get caught though? Mrs Weaver'll go completely ballistic."

"So?" Kenny shrugged. "What can she do? She can't put us in detention!"

"She could stop us going to the beach every day," Rosie pointed out.

"She could make us sit in our rooms and do schoolwork," Lyndz chimed in.

"She could send us home on the next plane," I added.

"Oh, and she could ban us from going on *any* other school trip *ever*," Fliss finished off.

"All right, all right," Kenny muttered, wrinkling her bright pink nose. "We'll just have to make sure we don't get caught then, won't we?"

As we went out of the canteen, Maria, Pilar, Isabella, Anna and Elena were just coming in, and they all grinned nastily at us.

"What a sad thing your teacher catch you last night!" Maria giggled, and then they all started talking in Spanish.

"It really bugs me when they do that!" Kenny said crossly, as we stalked past them with our noses in the air. "I wish I could understand what they're saying!"

"Well, I did try to teach you some Spanish, but you weren't interested!" I pointed out.

Kenny sighed. "I want to know how to say 'Shut up, you're totally getting on my nerves', *not* 'Do you want a carrot?'"

"What're we doing today?" Fliss asked. "Are we going to the beach again?"

"Yeah, but just for the morning," Rosie said. "It's free time, so we can do what we want."

"Excellent!" said Lyndz. "I reckon we should keep right away from those Spanish girls *and* from Mrs Weaver all day!"

We all thought that was a good idea, so

when we got to the beach, we bagged a couple of parasols as far away from everyone else as we could, and spread out our towels underneath them.

"I've got to keep my nose out of the sun," Kenny said, arranging herself so that the bottom half of her body was in the sun and her face was in the shade. "It's so red, it's glowing!"

"Yeah, you won't need to use your bedside lamp if you want to read at night!" I remarked, lying face down on my towel.

"Yee-argh!" I leapt up again as Kenny slapped some ice-cold sun cream on my back, and the others giggled. Although what had happened the night before had been a bit of a downer, we'd all cheered up again.

"I don't believe it!" Fliss suddenly screeched.

"What?" We all sat up.

"That Isabella's got the same swimsuit on as me *again*!" Fliss howled, looking outraged.

The Spanish girls were with their teacher

quite a way down the beach from us, but we could still see that Isabella was wearing the same costume as Fliss – a bright blue one-piece with pink flowers on it.

"It's not funny!" Fliss groaned as we tried not to laugh.

"Maybe you'd better go and ask her if she has loads of clothes, and likes fluffy toys!" Kenny said with a grin.

"And weddings!" Rosie added.

"She's nothing like me at all!" Fliss sniffed. She was starting to get wound up, so we dropped it.

After we'd sunbathed for a bit, we went down to the sea, and splashed around. We met up with some German girls who were staying at the holiday complex too, and they were brilliant. We didn't do any serious swimming because we felt too lazy, but we had a great time.

"I don't know why anyone goes on holiday in England when they could come here!" I sighed, floating on my back in the warm water. "If we were at home now, we'd be running in and out of the freezing sea, waiting for the rain to stop!"

"Hey, stop knocking England!" Rosie said. "It's not so bad."

"Yeah, we've got Walkers cheese and onion crisps!" Lyndz pointed out. "*And* Buckingham Palace!"

"We've got the best pop groups," Fliss joined in.

"And don't forget Leicester City FC!" Kenny added.

"OK, OK! I get your point, but you've got to admit, Spain's got better weather!" I dived under the water, and tried to grab Kenny's legs.

Kenny jumped out of my grasp. "Last one back to the parasols has to kiss Ryan Scott!" she yelled, and we all legged it out of the sea, and up the beach. Guess who was last.

"Oh, bad luck, Fliss," Kenny said sarcastically, as we waited for her to catch us up. "You lost."

Fliss turned pink, but then she frowned. "Hey, what's happened to my bag?"

All of Fliss's stuff was scattered across her towel, and her pink-and-white-striped beach bag was lying on its side.

"Hey, d'you think someone's been nicking our money?" Kenny gasped, grabbing her own bag.

Fliss, who was quickly going through her things, shook her head. "No, it's all here, my purse and everything. My bag must've just fallen over—" Then she stopped. "Hang on a minute. My sleepover diary's gone!"

"Are you sure?" Rosie asked, as Fliss rooted frantically through her belongings again.

"Certain sure!" Fliss said, tipping her bag upside-down and shaking it. "I know I put it in when I packed it this morning!"

We all searched the area around our parasols, picking up our towels and looking underneath, and checking our own bags, but the diary was nowhere to be seen.

Fliss was gradually turning as white as a ghost. "Where can it be?" she wailed. "I've got to get it back! It's got all our sleepover secrets in it!"

"Just a minute," Kenny said slowly, "you don't think *they've* nicked it, do you?"

"Who?" I asked, not realising for a second whom Kenny meant.

Kenny pointed down the beach at Maria and the others. "I reckon it's just the kind of thing they'd do! And they've had plenty of time while we were in the sea."

"I know they're pretty gross, but I don't think they'd go through our bags," Lyndz said doubtfully.

"Well, they wouldn't have to, would they?" Kenny pointed out triumphantly. "If Fliss's bag had fallen over and her stuff was lying there, all they'd have to do is pick the diary up!"

Fliss was now looking more green than white. "B– but there's everything about the Sleepover Club in there!" she stammered. "And – well…"

"What?" Kenny asked grimly. "Spit it out, Fliss."

"There's stuff about Mrs Weaver," Fliss

muttered, "*and* Ryan Scott."

"If they've nicked that diary, we'll be in heaps of trouble when they read it!" I said urgently. "We've got to find out if they've got it or not – and fast!"

CHAPTER EIGHT

"It's not here!" Fliss wailed, standing in the middle of the wrecked bedroom. We'd tipped out the entire contents of hers and Rosie's and Lyndz's bags, and we'd emptied the wardrobe. We'd even stripped the beds. But we hadn't found a sausage.

"What am I going to do?" Fliss moaned. "I'm dead if anyone reads that diary!"

"We're *all* dead," Kenny pointed out. "*Everyone's* going to know about our sleepovers."

"My membership card's tucked inside it too," Fliss muttered dismally.

"Oh, great, we might as well just invite everyone in the whole world to join the Sleepover Club!" Kenny said crossly. "We're not going to have any secrets left!"

"Cool it, Kenny!" I said as Fliss bit her lip, looking upset. "We still don't know where the diary is. Fliss might have dropped it somewhere."

"Yeah, but that means *anyone* could get their hands on it!" Lyndz said gloomily. "What if one of the kids from our school finds it?"

Fliss turned pale. "If Ryan Scott reads my diary, I'm going home on the next plane!"

"And what about Alana Banana?" Rosie said. "She might find it and keep it to show the M&Ms!"

We all looked at each other in silent horror. Things were going from bad to worse. We had to get that diary back or the Sleepover Club would be finished, and Fliss would die of embarrassment every time she saw Ryan Scott.

The sound of giggling behind us made us

turn round. Maria, Pilar and the others were standing in the corridor, laughing and pointing at us.

Kenny clenched her fists. "Right!" she announced. "I'm going to ask them straight out if they've got Fliss's diary, and if they have, I'm going to make them give it back!"

"Don't be an idiot, Kenny!" I hissed, grabbing her arm as she lunged forward. "If they *haven't* got it, they might go looking for it!"

Kenny stopped in mid-charge. "I hadn't thought of that."

"What do you look for?" Pilar called, as the other girls sniggered. "Something important?"

"Mind your own business!" Fliss snapped.

The Spanish girls went off, still laughing, and we all looked at one another.

"So d'you think they've got it or not?" Lyndz asked.

"I dunno," Kenny said with a frown, "but if they have, I bet they're going to make us sweat a bit before they give it back."

"Well, until we find the diary, everything's on hold," I said. "We can't have a sleepover in case they tell Mrs Weaver what we 'e planning. She'll go off her head if she catches us again."

We all looked gloomy.

"Well, I'm not sitting round here doing nothing!" Kenny raced over to the door.

"Where're you going?" Rosie asked, alarmed.

"To search their room!" And Kenny dashed off down the corridor.

"Kenny! Wait!" I yelled, but she ignored me.

"What's she playing at?" Fliss gasped, as we ran after her. "She'll be in big trouble if she gets caught!"

"The biggest," I said grimly, skidding to a halt outside the Spanish girls' room, just as Kenny closed the door behind her.

"What're you doing?" Rosie hissed, sticking her foot in it. "Get out of there!"

"I'm only going to have a quick look." Kenny hurried across the room, and started looking in the bedside lockers. "It's not like I'm going to *nick* anything."

"How come they've got a room for five people?" Fliss grumbled, looking round her. "If we had this room, we could have sleepovers every night!"

Suddenly Lyndz froze. "Someone's coming!" she hissed.

"Quick, under the beds!" Kenny ordered us.

We all flung ourselves down onto the carpet, and each rolled under one of the beds. Rosie rolled under the same one as me, so I had to shove her out of the way. She'd only just hidden herself under the next bed, when the door opened, and the Spanish girls came in.

We all lay there as still as statues, hardly daring to breathe. The girls were walking round the room, chatting in Spanish, and all I could see of them was their shoes. They kept coming right up to the beds, and then walking away again. At one point Maria's trainers were only about a millimetre from my nose.

Then, all of a sudden, they went out again and closed the door. I gave a sigh of relief, and rolled out from under the bed. The others did the same.

"Right, now we're getting out of here!" I said, glaring at Kenny and daring her to disagree.

"Oh, we might as well have a quick look now we're here—" Kenny began. But we didn't give her a chance to finish. We surrounded her, and frog-marched her out of the room.

"So what happens now?" Rosie asked, when we were safely outside.

"Not a lot," I said. "We can't do anything until we find that diary, so we'd better get looking."

We spent most of that afternoon searching for the diary around the holiday complex. The threat of those Spanish girls, or Mrs Weaver, or Alana Banana, or Ryan Scott getting hold of it was hanging over us all the time. It was a real downer because none of us could relax and enjoy ourselves until we knew where the diary was.

We didn't have a chance to look for it the following day, though, because our group, along with some of the German and Danish kids, went on a day trip to Barcelona. Pilar, Maria and the rest of their gruesome gang didn't come, so we got away from them for a while.

Barcelona was *excellent*. There were loads of interesting buildings, including a really weird-looking cathedral, a palace, big gardens and parks, a harbour, and streets and streets of interesting shops. We also saw a ginormous statue of Christopher Columbus, which had a lift inside so that you could ride right up to his head and look out over the whole city. We all wanted to go up it, until Mrs Weaver told us that about twenty years ago his head had fallen off! Then we weren't so keen.

We were taken to all the cultural places first, and then we were allowed to go shopping. That was the best bit! The shops were radical, and we all went mad and bought loads of stuff. Fliss and Rosie both got fans, and we all bought castanets, as well as presents for our families.

"That was ace!" Rosie sighed as we climbed back onto the minibus at the end of the day. "I love my castanets!"

As soon as we sat down, we all got our castanets out, and started clicking them and shouting "*Olé!*", until Mrs Weaver gave us a look from the front of the minibus.

"What's in that bag, Kenny?" Fliss asked curiously, pointing to a paper bag sticking out of Kenny's pocket.

Kenny put her hand in the bag, and pulled out a box of stinkbombs. We all stared at it.

"Where did you get those?" Lyndz asked.

"I nipped into a joke shop while you were looking at the fans." Kenny grinned. "I just thought they might come in handy."

"What for?" Fliss looked blank.

"Oh, get a life, Fliss!" Kenny said impatiently. "For those Spanish girls, of course. I reckon we should stinkbomb them every night until they give the diary back!"

We all started to laugh.

"Kenny, you're not serious!" I raised my eyebrows.

"'Course I am!" Kenny retorted. "I'm going to sneak down to their room tonight, and chuck a stinkbomb through their door!"

That wiped the smiles off our faces.

"You must be mad!" Fliss gasped. "It's miles too risky!"

"What if Mrs Weaver's on the prowl and catches you?" Rosie pointed out.

"It's not worth the hassle, Kenny," Lyndz advised her.

"Oh yes it is!" Kenny looked stubborn. "I'm well fed up with them taking the mickey out of us all the time, and I'm going to do something about it!"

"But they might not even have the diary!" Fliss wailed.

Kenny shrugged. "Who cares about the diary? I just wanna teach them a lesson!" She looked round at us. "So, are you coming with me? Or are you all a bunch of wimps?"

CHAPTER NINE

"Frankie!" Kenny leant over and shook my shoulder. I woke up with a start. "Time to go."

"OK," I said reluctantly, pushing back the duvet. We'd all tried to talk Kenny out of her crazy idea, but she wasn't having any of it. And we couldn't let her go on her own, could we? The Sleepover Club had to stick together, even though we would all be in deepest doom for the next million years if Mrs W caught us red-handed.

We went quietly over to the door. I was kind of wishing that Alana Banana would wake up, and then we wouldn't be able to go. But she was dead to the world, as usual, snoring like a foghorn.

Kenny turned off the corridor light, just to be on the safe side, and we tiptoed down to the others' room. It was pitch black without the lights on. We had our torches with us, but we didn't want to use them unless we had to, so we felt our way along the wall until we got to the right door.

"Here we are," Kenny whispered, her hand on the door handle. She flicked the torch on just to check, then quickly turned it off again. "Oh, rats, that's number eight – Mrs Weaver's room!"

"Oh, nice one, Kenny!" I groaned.

We hurried on to number seven. The others sat up in bed as we went in.

"All set?" Kenny asked breezily.

"Hang on a sec." Rosie leant over and picked something up off Fliss's bedside locker. "Guess what we've found!"

"Fliss's diary!" Kenny gasped. "Where was it?"

"Under my bed," Fliss muttered, looking highly embarrassed. "It must've fallen out of my bag."

"Oh, great!" I said crossly. "All that worrying for nothing!"

"So we don't have to go and let off the stinkbomb now, do we?" Lyndz pointed out, and I've got to admit, I felt pretty relieved.

"Are you *kidding*?" Kenny said fiercely. "They threw our clothes into that tree, remember? Anyway, I spent 300 pesetas on these stinkbombs, and I'm not going to waste them! Now, come on!"

Fliss, Rosie and Lyndz climbed out of bed reluctantly. They looked as nervous as I was feeling, but none of us was going to let Kenny down.

Kenny opened the door, and Fliss gave a little squeal.

"What's the matter?" Kenny hissed, alarmed.

"It's completely black out there!" Fliss muttered. "I'm going to get my torch."

Kenny grabbed her arm. "No, it's too

risky. We'll be safer in the dark."

"But how're we going to find our way?" Fliss wailed.

"We'll all stay in a line behind Frankie, and keep close to the wall," Kenny told her.

"Oh, great!" I grumbled. "Looks as though I'm in front again, as usual!"

We all got into a line – me at the front, followed by Kenny, Rosie, Lyndz and Fliss – and we linked hands. Then we shuffled out into the dark corridor.

Once we'd got past Mrs Weaver's room, we began to breathe more easily, but it was still a long way to the Spanish girls' room. I led everybody slowly down the corridor, feeling my way along the wall, until we came to the corner.

Suddenly, someone behind me hiccuped. Although it wasn't very loud, it *sounded* loud in the dead silence. My heart beating fit to bust, I yanked on Kenny's hand, and pulled everyone round the corner with me. We all flattened ourselves against the wall, and waited for the lights to go on. But nothing happened.

"Lyndz, you idiot!" I whispered. "Why didn't you hold your breath?"

"It wasn't me!" Lyndz whispered back indignantly.

"Well, who was it then?"

No one answered.

"Maybe this is going to be like a horror film," Kenny said, "and the monster'll join the end of the line and bump us off one by one."

"I'm not standing at the end then!" Fliss said, alarmed, trying to push in between Rosie and Lyndz.

"Ssh, we're here now anyway," I said.

Kenny flicked the torch on quickly to check that it was the right room, and then she crept across the corridor.

"Turn the torch off before you open the door!" I told her, but Kenny shook her head.

"I want to make sure I chuck the stinkbomb right into the middle of the room!" she said, taking the box out of her pyjama pocket.

We all watched breathlessly as Kenny opened the door, dimming the torch by putting her hand over the beam. *Then* we all nearly dropped down dead, as suddenly she flung the door wide open.

"What're you doing?" I gasped, my heart in my mouth.

"They're not here!" Kenny said crossly. "Look!"

She shone the torch round the room, and we all peered in. Every one of the beds was empty!

"Well, where are they then?" Rosie said, but we didn't get a chance to discuss it. Someone was opening the door of a room further down the corridor...

"Quick!" I hustled everyone into the room. "Get into the beds!"

We each dived into one of the empty beds, and lay there silently, pretending to be asleep. We saw the corridor light go on, then, the very next second, the door opened, and Miss Moreno, the Spanish girls' teacher, looked in. She said something in

Spanish, which was probably "Are you asleep?" and then, when nobody answered, she went out.

We all sat up, breathing huge sighs of relief. But that didn't last long because the next moment we heard Mrs Weaver's voice outside the door. We nearly died.

"Yes, I'm sure I heard someone moving around too," Mrs Weaver was saying. "Have you checked up on all your kids?"

"Not all of them," Miss Moreno said. "I will go and look at the rest now."

"Well, I'd better go and see if mine are all present and correct too," Mrs Weaver said grimly, and we all gasped. Now we were *really* in for it.

"What're we going to do?" Fliss moaned. "Mrs Weaver'll see we're not in our rooms!"

"She might not notice," Lyndz said hopefully.

"Maybe we ought to try and make it back," Rosie suggested.

"Oh yeah, and run slap-bang into Mrs Weaver as soon as we put one foot outside the door!" Kenny pointed out. "We're better off waiting here."

"We could pretend we'd just gone to the loo or something," I said.

"What, all five of us?" Rosie raised her eyebrows. "She'd never swallow that!"

We couldn't decide what to do, so we just stayed where we were, and waited. After a couple of minutes, Mrs Weaver and Miss Moreno came back down the corridor, and we strained our ears to hear what they were saying.

"Well, I can't understand it." Mrs Weaver spoke first. "I know I heard something. But all my pupils are safely tucked up in bed."

That floored us. *We* weren't in bed – well, not in our own beds anyway – but Mrs Weaver didn't seem to have noticed. Anyway, we didn't much care – it looked like we'd got away with it!

We waited for about fifteen minutes to let the teachers get back to sleep again, then we made a break for it. There wasn't much point in letting off the stinkbomb with no one there, so it had all been a waste of time really. *And* we were lucky we hadn't got rumbled by Mrs W...

"Let's get out of here!" Kenny said to our relief, flicking off the corridor light again.

"Can't we keep the lights on?" Fliss wailed.

"No way!" Kenny retorted. "If Mrs Weaver busts us, at least we've got a fighting chance of getting away in the dark!"

We set off. We were so nervous about not making a sound, we were even trying not to *breathe*.

As we inched our way along the corridor wall, I put my hand out, feeling for the corner, which I knew was coming up soon.

And I nearly passed out with shock when my hand touched someone else's fingers...

CHAPTER TEN

I don't know how I stopped myself from screaming, but I did. And if you've ever bumped into someone in the dark unexpectedly and felt their *flesh*, you'll know just how scary it is. I froze right there, but the others kept on coming and bumped into me.

"What's going on?" Fliss squealed.

I groped around for the nearest light switch and turned it on. There in front of us were the Spanish girls – Pilar at the front, with Maria and Isabella behind her and the twins at the back.

"What are *you* doing here?" Pilar and I said furiously right at the same moment.

None of us knew what to say. We didn't know whether to be relieved it wasn't one of our teachers, or annoyed that it was them, so we all stood there looking stupidly at each other, and shuffling our feet.

"We've – er – just been to the bathroom," Rosie said weakly.

"You go the wrong way then," said Maria, jerking a thumb over her shoulder. "The bathroom is this way."

"Well, where've *you* been?" Kenny shot back. "I bet you went to our rooms to play a trick on us!"

The Spanish girls looked embarrassed.

"What a shame we weren't there then!" Fliss said triumphantly.

"So, where were you?" Maria asked suspiciously. "I think *you* also try to play a trick on *us*!"

This time it was our turn to look embarrassed.

"We must've passed each other in the

corridor!" I said. "Did you hiccup?"

Elena turned pink. "I do that."

"She hiccup all the time!" Maria explained.

"That sounds just like someone I know!" I glanced at Lyndz. "Anyway, we saved your necks when your teacher came in to check on you, 'cos we were in your beds, pretending to be you!"

"*So?*" said Pilar. "Your teacher come to check on *you* also – and we did same thing!"

"You mean, you were in *our* beds and we were in *yours*?" Fliss gasped.

"What about Alana Banana?" I asked. "Didn't she notice?"

"You mean that girl who sound like a pig?" Maria grinned. "No, she not wake up!"

We all looked at each other. Then we started to giggle. The Spanish girls *were* just like us, after all. Suddenly our big war seemed really stupid and how we had all been creeping around each other's rooms seemed really funny. We tried to stop laughing, but we couldn't.

"You come to our room!" Maria mouthed

at us, so we all hurried silently back down the corridor to their bedroom. Once we were inside, though, we all collapsed onto the beds, shaking with laughter.

"I can't believe Alana Banana didn't notice what was going on!" Kenny was lying on Maria's bed, stuffing a corner of the duvet into her mouth to muffle her giggles. "That girl's so dozy, she'd forget her own name!"

"Is this her real name – Alana Banana?" Anna said in a serious voice.

That cracked the Sleepover Club up.

"Why do you laugh?" Anna said, looking a bit prickly like Rosie does sometimes.

So we quickly explained about the M&Ms, and about Alana. If I was a beanpole like Pilar, and Kenny and Maria were totally alike, and Lyndz and Elena both got the hiccups, then Anna was definitely a bit like Rosie!

"So, what trick you try to play on us?" Maria asked curiously.

Kenny pulled the box of stinkbombs out of the pocket of her pyjamas, and held it up.

"And us!" said Maria, and she did exactly the same thing.

"Maybe *that* would have woken Alana Banana up!" Rosie suggested, and set us all off laughing again.

When we'd finally stopped giggling, we sat there looking at each other in silence. It felt a bit weird. I mean, we'd been enemies for the last three days, and now here we were, getting on like great mates.

"I very sorry I say English football teams are not good," Maria said suddenly.

"And I'm sorry I thought you'd taken my bag!" Kenny added immediately.

"I'm sorry I tipped you off your surfboard," Lyndz said to Elena.

"And I am sorry we throw your clothes in the tree," Pilar told us.

"Right, so we're all sorry about *everything*," I said. "Let's talk about something else now!"

"You want some Coca-Cola?" Pilar took some cans out of her bedside locker. "We have crisps also."

"Hey, this is just like being at a sleepover!"

Rosie said.

"Sleep over? What is this?" Anna asked, looking interested.

"You know. *Dormir sobre*," I said. "At least I think that's what they're called in Spanish."

"Ah, you mean like a pyjama party," laughed Pilar. "We have them sometimes too."

I nodded. "Yeah, kind of, but we have *special* ones. We're the Sleepover Club!"

"I do not understand. What is that?" Maria asked.

"It's a secret, but we could tell you a bit about it, if you really wanted to know…" I glanced at Rosie, Kenny, Fliss and Lyndz, and they all nodded.

So I told them about how the Sleepover Club had started, and they were really into all that. Then I told them about our sleepover song and our membership cards and the midnight feasts. We don't usually go round telling everyone our secrets, but they promised they wouldn't breathe a word about it to anyone. So then we started telling them about some of the adventures we'd had during our sleepovers, and soon we were all crying with laughter.

"What do you say? Will *we* have one of these Sleepover Clubs?" Pilar said, looking at Maria, Elena, Anna and Isabella.

"Yeah, why don't you?" Kenny said eagerly. "We'll help you to organise it!"

"Hey, why don't we have one of our sleepovers right now?" I suggested. "Then we can show you exactly what we do!"

Everyone thought that was a great idea, so we all got into the beds, the Spanish girls at the tops, and the Sleepover Club at the bottoms. We finished off the crisps and the Coca-Cola, and then Maria gave everyone some chocolate. We started off by telling jokes, and then they taught us some Spanish. After that, we told horror stories. Maria was just as good at that as Kenny was, and between them they nearly frightened Fliss and Isabella to death.

Then we showed them some of the dance routines we'd worked out, and they showed us how to flamenco. We had a brilliant time, and it was nearly three o'clock in the morning before we all started yawning.

"I think Sleepover Club is fantastic idea!" Isabella said sleepily.

"So do you think you'll start one yourselves?" I asked.

The Spanish girls nodded.

"Tomorrow you are going to the beach, yes?" Pilar asked. "If you like, we play volleyball together?"

"You bet!" Kenny said eagerly. "See you in the morning!"

So everything turned out fine in the end. We spent the rest of the week going round with Pilar, Maria, Elena and the others, and guess what? We had a sleepover every night – yeah, *every night*! That was a bit of a record even for us!

On the last night we had a really special sleepover. The teachers were having a party themselves and they'd agreed that just this once we could go into each other's rooms.

So, because we could make as much noise as we liked, we showed the Spanish girls how to play all our International Gladiators games.

We'd had such a good time in Spain, I didn't really want to go home. But in another way, I did. You know what it's like – all your mum and dad do is nag nag nag when you're at home, then when you go away, you can't wait to see them again! And I was *really* missing Pepsi.

"Back home to boring old Cuddington!" Kenny sighed, as we climbed onto the minibus. "I wish we could've stayed for another week!"

"Me too," Fliss said, waving at Pilar and the others who'd come to see us off.

"It's a shame we didn't have long to get to know them," Rosie said gloomily, waving too. "D'you realise we'll probably never see them again in the whole of our lives?"

That made us all feel pretty gruesome.

"Everyone here?" Mrs Weaver hurried down the bus with her clipboard, checking us off one by one. "Right, I think we're just about ready to leave."

We all stood up and opened the windows.

"'BYE!" we yelled. "*Adiós*! Write and tell us about your sleepovers!"

"We will!" they called back, and we all waved until we couldn't see each other any more.

"Have you had a good time?" Mrs Weaver asked us as the minibus headed towards the airport. "I noticed you were getting very friendly with some of the Spanish girls." She smiled. "Well, towards the end of the week, anyway!"

We all turned a bit pink.

"I thought you might like to know that Miss Moreno and I have been talking about making exchange visits between our schools," Mrs Weaver went on. "We'd go to visit their school in Madrid, and they'd come to ours in Cuddington. What do you think?"

We all sat up.

"That sounds excellent, Miss!" Kenny said